The Lion of Ackbarr

Book One

The Medici Chronicles

Erme Lander

Cover image – www.redhoudinidesign.wordpress.com/

ISBN 978-1-9997453-4-9

More frog than princess, Erme Lander lives in
Gloucestershire with her two children and a mad cat.

Other books by Erme lander available on Amazon

The Vampire Duology

A Dark Inheritance
A Dark Infection

The Medici Chronicles

The Lion of Ackbarr
Blood Lore
Medici of Ackbarr
Blood Debt
Warlord of Ackbarr

Lord of Dust
Death's Touch
Sasha
Willow

Table of Contents

Chapter 1

The house was still and quiet with grief. Both her parents were tense, with new lines ageing their faces. No one would tell her what had happened and question after question had been refused an answer. Her father's patience cracked when she stormed and shouted her frustration and he snapped back in a whiplash demand for her to behave.

Unused to the discipline, she refused to calm and her father ordered her to be locked into her room, stating the time had come for her to behave like the lady she was supposed to be. Her younger brother and sisters watched big eyed from the corners as two of the servants with embarrassed faces did as they were ordered. Not believing her banishment, she screamed and kicked at the door until she was exhausted.

Mika threw herself on the bed and wept. Her brother was gone. Her twin, the person she'd learned to walk and read with, they'd learnt everything together. He'd taught her how to fight when her father had refused, had taught her how to read when it wasn't fashionable for a woman to have any education except how to run a household. Taught her until finally laughing, her father had given in and allowed her the same freedoms, the same tutors, running around in the same clothes until the only way anyone could tell them apart was by the length of her hair.

Kaylan had been supposed to lead them all when her father died. Encouraged and cosseted as the jewel of the family. Confident and outgoing, everyone had loved him. He'd been fifteen and full of an easy arrogance to go with their father to a city in a foreign country. So full of himself that she'd ended up filling his bed with kava flour. The yells that had ensued that night, she choked with remembered laughter through her tears. She'd been soundly scolded for wasting the servants time and he'd still spent the night wriggling, trying to escape the itch. Not so arrogant the morning after, he'd lost no time in dunking her in the horse trough. The guards had watched, amused at first and finally yelling their encouragement as she'd fought to pull him in with her. Until her mother had arrived, tight lipped, and the guards had abruptly found other duties to do. She and Kaylan had hung their heads, both soaked to the skin and smiling sideways at each other through the telling off.

Now no one would say what had happened. She couldn't believe he'd died and not knowing if he was dead or disappeared was horrendous. The shared looks between her parents, her mother's closed eyes and face tight with pain. Mika stared at the moons, leaning against the frame of the open window, her eyes filling with tears. They blurred into a sea of silver and she buried her head in her arms.

Muffled talk from the garden roused her. Her father's voice saying, "I tried, there was nothing I could do…"

Sniffing, Mika leant further to peer around the deep walls of the window. The shutters frustrated her, partially closing off the view of the garden from the single storey house. She could just see her parents if she pulled all her weight onto her toes and leaned out.

"Even as Ambassador…" Her mother.

"We couldn't tell anyone. We had no credible reason to stay to look…" Her father's voice dropped lower, "...was there."

Her mother froze. Mika couldn't see her face, but she could see how she stood, hunted and wary. "Did he see you?" Who were they talking about now?

"Of course he saw me. He's attached himself to the King's retinue." Her father's voice was bitter.

She leaned further, fascinated. The King? They must be talking about someone in Ackbarr, someone they both knew. Ackbarr was many weeks travel away, over the mountains that surrounded Cassai. How would her mother know someone there? Her mother's quieter voice was inaudible over the rustling of leaves.

"I couldn't mention anything and he knows it. All he did was smirk."

Mika could see her father's shadow stretched thin in the clear night, his arms flung out in an impatient gesture, unlike his normal reserved self. She leaned further, trying not to be seen as she peered. The figures of her parents stood by the tiny stream, the indistinct shapes of the plants moving, blurring their black and silver outlines. Her mother's head was bowed and as her father went to her, she shook him off. She walked away fast and out of sight. Mika watched her father stand in the moonlight for a while, then he seemed to sigh and followed her mother inside.

Her mother came into her room the next morning. Swathed in her usual restrictive clothing, she sorted quietly through Mika's drawers. She selected suitable dresses for the day, then sat on her bed and stroked back Mika's hair while she lay there. Mika stared at the ceiling, refusing to speak, her eyes still swollen from the previous night. Her mother waited until Mika finally looked her way.

"You need to get dressed."

She was tall, with sandy hair and her skin pale from being inside, her emotions were contained like her clothing. Mika had heard stories about her youth. Head strong and stubborn, Ayanna still showed the occasional flash of temper when thwarted. At those times even her father gave way. Mika resembled her closely, the only difference being that her skin was tanned. She pulled herself up, looked at the clothes and groaned.

"Not today."

"Yes today." Her mother was firm. Mika knew that tone, no arguments. "We have a visitor."

"And?"

"He has come to see you. It was arranged while your father was away." Mika sat up straight. First her brother gone and now this?

Her mother stood to leave, "You will do us credit Mika. You will not shame us. Nothing is firm yet, but it is a good match."

That's why her mother had come and not a servant. A servant could be side stepped, her mother could not be. Mika watched her leave, shutting the door quietly behind her. Mika sighed and went to wash her face in the bowl left for her.

Mika entered her father's private entertaining rooms at midday. The rooms weren't familiar, she'd seldom had reason to enter them. It was a male room, everything functional yet still beautifully made. A few touches she recognised from her mother, the vase full of flowers from the garden, the slender hangings next to the door. To her surprise she spotted a piece of embroidery she'd done at a younger age, scowling her way through while wanting to be outside with Kaylan. The sun was shining out there now despite her brother not being here. It should be raining, the skies weeping as she wanted to. She pulled herself back from imagining what mischief they'd be planning if he hadn't disappeared.

She'd shortened her stride to accommodate her dresses, now correctly draped after several frustrating attempts and her hair pinned up under a stole. She paused by the door. Her father was expansively talking to another man by the fire. His gestures were wide, his face full of pride as he noticed her. The pain of yesterday had been put away for another time, not to be shared with strangers. A youth stood next to the man, hands behind his back, listening to the conversation.

They turned to look and dipped their heads in respect. Keeping her steps short, she demurely approached them, flicking her eyes up to look. The man was fat, he had thick lips, black curly hair and he sized her up like the trade deal she was. The younger man looked pleasant enough she supposed, a slimmer version of his father. She was struck by the differences between him and her brother. This youth was the same height as her. Her brother was taller, like both their parents. She corrected herself, was tall, had been tall.

"Mika, my daughter," her father introduced her. "Mika, this is Mekhi and his son Rylan." He spoke in Mekhi's language, his accent changed with the weight of different words. She understood him, she'd picked it up through Kaylan's tutors quickly enough, although her own speech was a little more stilted.

She bent her head to them, wrapped in her soft blue stole, her long dresses a little darker. Sitting close by, she listened while her father talked and watched them. The man was a trader, dealing in rich fabrics. He showed them samples of his wares and she brushed her fingers across them when offered. They were far different from the sober colours she was used to. She could tell by the feel that the fabric her dress was made of was just as good only less ostentatious.

Her father was also dressed simply, touches of silver thread gleamed at the collar and cuffs of his long tunic, his trousers tucked into calf high boots, it suited him. His earring winked in the sunlight, little jewellery needed for show. The trader boasted about his contacts, his dealings with the overseas far away from this little country. Her father listened, his face polite, he was an ambassador for this little country, well known for his own deals. Mika shifted, wondering why his son had been chosen, it was obvious that her father didn't like Mekhi. Nothing showed in his face or mannerisms, but to someone who knew him well…

Her mother came in, servants following with trays. Small cakes, sweetmeats, herbal teas and a tiny teapot on a tripod with a candle underneath to keep the brew warm. Ayanna supervised the servants, artfully arranging the sweets closer to the trader. Delicate gestures endeared the visitors to her and the atmosphere warmed. No one would know she rarely left the estate as she engaged Rylan in conversation over affairs in his homeland. Mika saw a rare public flash of adoration over her father's face, as he observed her while Mekhi had his snout in a cup.

Her mother sat the young man next to Mika. He had rings on his fingers and he fiddled with his embroidered cuffs. The fabric was stiff, pulled tight in places. Rylan sat as though expecting her to bite. A flash of rebellion was quelled by her mother's presence before it started, but she couldn't help wondering how much he'd squeal if she poked him. Her brother... she stopped herself, her brother wasn't here. She imitated her mother, head bowed slightly, voice quiet when she was spoken to.

Mekhi announced from his chair, "I believe this will be a good match Koren." He hadn't asked his son she noticed or referred to her father by his title, she squashed the indignation down. "I will be leaving within a twelve night. I would like everything wrapped up by that point. Your daughter can then come home with us."

Her father blinked in surprise, but kept his voice steady. "A twelve night? That is a little quick, people will talk."

The trader shrugged, "People are already talking. The passes will close shortly, I would prefer to have the arrangements sorted this side of winter."

For the first time her father looked unsure, then nodded. "Yes." Mika watched as they shook hands, sealing the deal, selling her. Her mother seemed as shocked as Mika, trapped within her own role. Her father and the two men walked out to his study to deal with the paperwork, leaving them together.

"Mother."

Her mother's lips thinned. "It is for the best." Mika opened her mouth to protest.

"No Mika. You cannot understand. In twelve days' time you will go with them. You will need to study how to behave and what they will expect. Their society is different from ours. You have had far more freedom than their daughters."

Her head was spinning. She'd never been out of the country before. The furthest she'd travelled was five miles away to her closest friend Alma and that was a long enough trek through the forests. She stood, chin up and icily refused to shout, pinning herself into the role they'd forced her into.

"May I leave the room?"

At her mother's nod she stalked out, hindered by her skirts. Tight with her own upset, she couldn't respond when she saw her mother's face drop into her hands as she shut the door.

Chapter 2

The twelve days passed in a flurry of packing, of sorting out old clothes and standing for the fitting of the new. So far to travel and so little could be taken. Mika had to make hard choices over cherished possessions. Her life was being compacted into a tiny space, stuffed until she felt ready to burst.

Mika was lost in all the preparations, hurtling from one appointment to another. She barely had time to stand in front of a window, let alone go out into the sunlight. Her mother spoke while the dressmakers fiddled with the fabric draped over Mika, pins poking her as she flinched from their attentions. Her words became a lecture to Mika's tired ears, speaking of how she should act and what was expected of her.

"They will expect you to be foreign, that does not mean you should embarrass us. Either in dress or in manners." Her mother was firm. "You are an ambassador's daughter. Remember it." Mika pulled a face, gazing out of the window at the blue green sky. Tiny clouds puffed past and she felt her body twitch in empathy.

Her mother pulled her thoughts back to the present. "Are you listening? You know there are problems between Ackbarr and Cassai, do not allow anyone to use them as an excuse." Mika rolled her eyes, if there were problems then why was she being married off to this boy? The threat of war from Ackbarr had been looming for years.

"Mekhi is well-known and respected in Fenin, you should be safe there if anything happens. Listen to what they say and watch how to behave." Her mother tugged at the plait she was weaving into Mika's hair, twisting it up with the ribbon while the dressmaker fussed with the hem around her feet, muttering to her apprentice.

Mika breathed out gustily and switched off as she gazed outside. She ached for time alone, to ride, run and laugh. The dressmakers ignored her mother talking and pulled at Mika's arms, murmuring requests to turn, to stand this way or that.

A knock at the door and Mika looked up, desperate for anything to distract her from the quiet lecture. She grinned in delight as her friend Alma stuck her head around the door and swayed, forgetting for a moment she wasn't allowed off the stool.

Her mother sighed, slid in a pin to keep the plait in place and left them. Alma sat close by, making comments with admiring eyes. Mika felt exposed on the stool and was relieved when she was finally allowed to step down and take the dress off. The dressmakers fussed over folding it carefully as Mika changed into older clothes.

"Is that your wedding dress?"

"No." She pulled Alma through the door into the corridor, escaping while she could. There'd be someone looking for her shortly. "That's just one of the dresses I'm having made." She pulled a face and imitated her mother, "I mustn't shame us." She tried to run her hands through her hair and started taking the plaits out in irritation.

"I thought you looked beautiful."

Mika stopped fiddling and stared. Alma's eyes were shining. "Alma, I'm marrying a boy I've met once. I'm leaving here and probably never coming back."

"Yes," Alma's voice was breathy, "He wants to marry you and take you away with him, just like we've talked about. Just imagine, the places you'll see. A different country, you'll be exotic there."

This wasn't right. Yes, they'd talked about eloping with boys. The usual romantic claptrap, but this was different, a trade deal. Alma was her best friend, her other friends had been friends with her brother as much as her. Running around with the children from the servants and estate workers, laughing and shouting in boisterous play. Alma had been the one to write to, share confidences with, now it looked like Mika was the one Alma was looking up to.

Mika checked around for servants. "Alma, I don't want to go." They stopped in the corridor, the daylight shaded as it came through the shutters in bars across the floor. "I don't have a choice in this. It's different to what we've spoken about. It's real." Tears started to rise.

Alma hugged her, "It's okay, you're probably nervous. I'd be in a dreadful state if it were me. Have you seen my new dress for the day? Come and see, it's not as nice as yours..." Alma pulled her down the corridor and sighing, Mika let her, tugging at the plaits as they went.

Rylan came at various points to make polite conversation. Despite her fluency in his language, her accent gave him problems, leaving gaps in the conversation. A small gift would be delivered, a cool kiss on the cheek when he left, nothing more. She gave him an equally reserved response, not knowing how to handle this boy who was going to be her husband. The urge to poke him still had to be contained, now it was overlaid by the dread of leaving home.

The conversation was stilted. Two strangers and they were never left alone to get to know each other better. Mika wondered what it was that they could do, they were going to be married in less than two weeks. Her mother said it was for appearances sake. Mika thought it was more likely to make sure she behaved herself.

Alma was constantly excited, talking about the wedding. Asking her questions about her new husband, many of which she couldn't answer. Telling Mika about all the things she would see, that she should write to her when she got to her new home. Mika found her chatter irritating, she knew Alma was hurt by her indifference, but she was almost glad when another appointment came to interrupt them.

When Rylan arrived one day Alma contrived to be around in the entrance hall so she could see him, and giggled behind her hand at Mika's formal greeting. Alma found Rylan fascinating, his dark hair, his bright blue eyes made her own sparkle with delight. Rylan in turn found it difficult to take his eyes off the creamy plait curling from underneath Alma's stole.

Mika watched everything as though in a dream, unsure of how it could be happening to her. She and Alma had spoken of marriage from time to time, most girls of her age did, but this was too sudden. She'd always assumed she'd marry a boy from her own country. It was a small population, spread out over distances. Boys would go looking for a bride from different parts of the country, it was accepted that they would work in a strange town or village while looking.

It was an adventure for most. The richer boys would have placements found for them, hints about a girl's suitableness made and the parents watching to make sure proprieties where observed. There were the occasional elopements, talked about in whispers of two lovers running away to live in the wilds until no one could dispute their marriage but these were rare in the strict society.

Still, she'd expected to marry one of her own. She couldn't even expect her mother to come and visit, Mika knew better than to ask. A few times a year her mother visited family, nothing else. Her father might come on the way to and from his duties, but that was it. A homesickness poured through her, twisting her stomach, stopping her eating.

Watching her one morning, picking at her food, her mother snapped at her father, "She needs to know something, we can not leave this." She turned back to Mika. "Your brother shamed us. I will not tell you the how, but it is partly our fault. You know that your father and I are related."

Mika nodded, they certainly looked alike and yet most people in their country looked similar. Tall and blonde with green or blue eyes, it was the norm for the small country. Her mother was unusual in having darker hair, like many of the royal family she was related to. Most were white blond like her father. Not many people took partners from outside the borders and until recently those borders had been closed.

"We should never have married." Her mother looked embarrassed, her father stared at the wall. "I forced the issue. We were allowed to stay together on the condition that our children would marry out of the country, to dilute the blood."

Mika stared, how could her brother shaming them be connected with their marriage?

"There are certain problems that arise when our people breed too closely Mika. We were not expecting it with your brother. He was old for it to happen. It has not been documented for so long... we had hoped..." Her voice trailed off. Composing herself again she carried on, "Mekhi has been good enough to look past your brother's disappearance, there are things even he does not know. He will get good contacts from your father and a handsome dowry for you. I am sorry it is happening so quickly, but it must."

"But what happened to Kaylan?" She was desperate to prise her fingers under her parent's imposed silence. "Why..."

Her mother's chin went up. "No more." The flash in her eye silenced her. Even Mika wasn't so wilful as to cross her mother in a temper. Mika ground her teeth, Alma had tried to get her to talk about her brother. She'd refused as flatly as her mother had now, given excuses not to talk. She didn't want to think that she might never see Kaylan again. She ached under her scab of indifference. She was followed by her father as she left the room.

"Please don't judge your mother by what she cannot tell you Mika." Her father's voice was soft.

"Why not?"

"Some things hurt too much, even now." He looked over his shoulder at the open door, a hopeless look in his face. Unprepared for her father's vulnerability, she twisted away from him and walked swiftly down the corridor, determined to hold onto her own upset.

She only had the deep night to herself. Alma slept in the room with her, bouncing with good intentions. Mika was often so tired she fell asleep immediately on hitting the pillow, cutting Alma off in mid-sentence. Despite that, her dreams were disturbed, those she could remember. Dreams of pacing through undergrowth, looking for something, her head swinging from side to side. The woods around her were full of life, everything in motion. All to be noted and filed, every sound, every rustle. She found herself looking forwards to sleeping, the only escape she had from being squeezed into the mould of bride and lady.

The wedding day came too soon for Mika. Tense with nerves, she woke early for once and tiptoed out of the room. Alma was breathing lightly, curled into a ball on her bed next to the wall. Mika slipped into the garden before the servants saw her, enjoying the respite. The sun had risen, the dew fresh on the grass and the wind rippling through the trees beyond. She was light headed, not believing this would be her last day here.

She'd dressed without thinking, slid into her old clothes, a tunic and trousers left over from her brother. They'd been stuffed into a pile under her bed, dusty from the weeks of not wearing them. She stretched her legs and revelled in the freedom to walk properly, not having to worry about how her dresses were draped and having them catch her stride.

Her boots became damp from the dew as she walked to her favourite spot, a bench close to the wall and she sat, enjoying the coolness. The sun's light warmed the red tiles of the house. The cook house's fire had just been lit, dark smoke hung in the air, misting the deeper green of the broad leafed forest behind. A sigh escaped her, the smell of grass, the calls and distant laughter of the guards changing over - home. Secure in the garden her mother tended, coaxing the plants to do their best in the poor soil. Vineflowers clambered and humped over the trellis fencing between the paths, a tiny stream sparkled around carefully placed boulders, the cream walls of the house and small deep windows. Tears prickled her eyes at the thought of leaving.

Leaning against the wall, she wondered what would happen if she climbed the wall and ran away. The idea tugged at her. It would be easy, the wall wasn't high. Leave this whole business behind, live as she wanted to. The idea expanded, filling the whole of her, becoming a longing, a desperation. To stride through the woods, like in her dreams, a tingling passed over her skin and she shivered.

The tugging ceased as she heard her mother call and the scent of the Vineflowers filled her nostrils. Her mother was looking for her. She stayed quiet. The consequences of running? Whilst she was headstrong, she wasn't stupid. She didn't know enough about surviving out there. She'd be found and brought back in disgrace. Whether she would marry after that, she didn't know but there would be punishment.

Mika sighed again and stood, she had to go through with this, maybe it wouldn't be so bad. He was good looking in his own foreign way, maybe they could learn to love one another or at least respect each other. Her mother saw her coming out and she realised from the unguarded expression on her face that similar thoughts had been running through her mother's head.

Expecting a scolding for being in her old clothes, she was surprised to receive a hug and have fingers run through her hair. "I will remember you like this. Do not forget yourself." Mika found the concept ominous considering she was expected to marry out and be someone she wasn't.

She was too nervous to eat much at lunch. They got ready for the ceremony slowly. Alma's laughter was forced at times. Mika's head was tight, aware that the time they had together was fast disappearing. Her little sisters sat on the bed, watching her with big eyes, a stranger in her new dresses.

At last mid-afternoon came. Her father arrived, looking impressive in his court uniform, not broad, but tall enough to appear imposing. Mika stared, she'd never seen him dressed so splendidly. He gave a smile at her surprise, held her hand and kissed her cheek.

Her mother checked her over one last time and nodded. She was dressed simply in contrast to Mika. Her darker hair, connecting her closely to the royal family, was enough to convey her status in a way that rich fabrics and jewellery could not. Her father offered his arm and walked Mika to the hall. It was decorated with boughs, a fire in the hearth, twined Vineflowers around the pillars – her mother's touch.

Mika stared in front of her, fingers gripping her father's arm as they walked, not wanting to see the priest and the few cousins waiting near the back of the hall. She concentrated on breathing, feeling light-headed. The trader and his son stood in their places by the priest. She spoke the words in a daze, heard Rylan say his part. The priest made the ritual cuts on each of their left hands and joined them together with a silken rope. The ceremony was brief and all to soon she belonged to someone else.

They moved to the inn where the trader was staying. More symbolic to Mika than the ceremony – she was no longer part of her own family. A meal in the evening, plenty of food, music and storytelling, most of it passed in a blur. The trader sat, fat and pleased, talking to her father and eating hugely. Faces swam in front of her, she gazed at the walls, nibbling at her food. Her new husband sat next to her, paid her attention by offering food and wine. She picked at the bandage covering her left hand. The small amount of wine she'd drunk had gone to her head and abruptly she wanted her mother. She couldn't see her. Mika looked around with blurring eyes and panic rising, where was she? Someone said something close by, she blinked and turned.

"Are you tired? Would you like to leave?" Mika hiccupped in surprise and Rylan smiled indulgently. Her husband. She nodded, she wanted to get out of here, run away and be somewhere quiet where she could think. He stood proudly, offered his elbow and walked her out, flushing to the cheers of the guests.

The upstairs was cool and dim. The best room had been set aside for them, more luxurious than any of her parent's rooms. Her eyes lost themselves in the furnishings. Unused to the richness, Mika was pleased her father had insisted on the wedding ceremony being at their house and not in this strange place. She jumped. A mouth on hers, hands pulling at her clothing, trying to find a way in. Not rough, but insistent. Numb, she obediently helped him and refused to think about what was happening to her body.

She lay in bed afterwards, she needed a wee. Rylan was sprawled with an arm across her. Mika slid out, went to the privy and cleaned herself. He disturbed as she got back in, pulled her close, muttering sleepily. She stared at the canopy as he settled down having reassured himself that she was still there. Her body wasn't her own, or her life.

Mika supposed the man and wife thing hadn't been too bad. It had been business-like, a brisk transaction that she felt she'd come worse off in and with the faint sense of injustice she wondered if that was all there was to it.

She twisted slightly, aching inside. She hadn't expected this feeling of being used and owned by someone. Alma had asked about it and she'd brushed her off, not wanting to think too closely. She'd been aware of the mechanics for years, seen animals and her brother had always been talking to his friends about this maid or that. Her brother. Tears rose and she cried quietly into her pillow. Lost, both her brother and her family. She sought solace in her dreams, running through the dark forests.

Chapter 3

In the morning she was allowed to get up after he'd had his way again. Mika hesitantly tried for a bit more enthusiasm this time and he'd looked a little puzzled at her attempts. A discreet knock and murmur announced breakfast had been laid in the other room.

Breakfast was awkward. He was still a stranger, albeit one who had knowledge of her body. She nibbled a few slices of fruit and drank water. She watched as he ate heartily and wondered how long it would take for him to get as large as his father. She imagined him that size and on top of her and put the slice of fruit down.

"You should eat more." Mika jumped. "There's nothing to you. You should eat." He gestured to the table. She shook her head, she'd never been a breakfast person. "You will be hungry later, we will be travelling far today."

"How far?"

Rylan looked flustered, "A long way, further than you've ever been. You will ride in the cart like a lady."

How did he know how far she'd been? Anyway, she'd rather ride. Mika nearly snapped at him, then closed her mouth, remembering her mother. She had to behave, she was a married woman now. There was an uncertain look in his eye, he'd caught the flash of temper and she hurriedly asked about the journey, thinking of questions he shouldn't have any problems in answering. Allowed to demonstrate his superior knowledge, he calmed, beginning to boast about the deals and fabrics they'd gathered so far.

Downstairs, Mekhi was complaining about the state of his head in between giving orders to the mule drivers and guardsmen. Rylan left her at the door to stand next to his father while he grumbled over the chaos. Mika looked around at the milling animals and people in the courtyard feeling the panic rise again. She was leaving, and without a chance to say goodbye.

She caught a flash of familiar house colours – her father's guards, and was swept into her mother's embrace before she could think. Her mother carefully wiped her eyes with the edge of her own stole and arranged Mika's scarf closer over her face. "You will remember?" Mika nodded, she was a grown up, she had to behave. She cuddled her little brother and sisters close before standing to hug her father.

He pulled her into his arms, looking worried and proud, "You look like your mother when I first met her." Her smile trembled and he walked her over to Rylan. "She will ride today." Rylan looked surprised. Her smile widened, with her father giving the orders they would not dare disagree.

With yet more grumbling from Mekhi, a small pony was found and an awkward looking side saddle put on. Rylan helped her on as though she were made of glass and fussed over placing her foot in the stirrup. Mika saw the gleam of amusement in her father's eyes. He knew of the time she'd ridden the stud owned by the family neighbouring their fields, with nothing more than a halter line on for a bet with her brother. He also knew about the beating Kaylan had received from the owner and taken without complaint because of the mistaken identity. He knew she was more capable of riding the feisty horses ridden by their guardsmen than her husband. She kept her mouth shut and accepted the help.

Mika waved goodbye as they finally moved off. A train of mules followed them piled high with rolls of material and the cart with her baggage. She twisted to keep waving and her last glimpse was of her mother burrowing her face into her father's shoulder as they turned to walk back to the inn.

The side-saddle gave her backache. She desperately wanted to get rid of it, even riding bareback was better than this. The pony was gentle, needing little guidance from her as it trotted along with the other horses. Patches of shade and sunshine dotted the road. Mika strained to hear the birds calling and the breeze rustling the leaves above the bellowing of the mules in the train. She gazed into the forest, trying to spot any of the shy wildlife. Rylan mistook her interest for concern. When he told her that she didn't need to worry about wild animals, she nearly snorted with laughter. Nothing would come near them with the amount of noise they were making.

After the morning's ride she was pleased to stop for lunch. Mekhi made noises about her travelling in the cart, riding a horse was not a fit occupation for a married woman as far as he was concerned. Taking a deep breath, Mika smiled and agreed. She tolerated the jouncing around while looking at the countryside. Her back continued to ache, a deep pain from sitting straight and not fidgeting. Even her mother rode astride when travelling, wearing wide legged trousers and boots, she was as capable and tough as Mika when she chose to be.

Both riding side saddle and sitting in the cart were uncomfortable, she was starting to see why Fenin women didn't travel. Thick forest surrounded them, rich and vivid, similar to her dreams the previous night. She gazed around to distract herself, storing up the views to add to her night time excursions.

It took several days of travelling to reach the mountain border, staying at the finest inns and being looked after wherever they ended up. Mekhi would announce himself to the innkeeper as they arrived. He expected the best of everything, allowed himself to be pampered and came down late every morning with an aching head. Rylan followed his father's example, coming late to their bed and waking her with his clumsy intentions.

Mika knew her father always insisted on travelling quietly, with no fuss and dealing with his own horses, not expecting his guards to do anything that he wouldn't. He considered it a mark of pride that he could keep up with any of his guards, even to the point of sleeping rough if he had to. She, on the other hand was treated as though she were delicate. A porcelain cup, to be admired as something important, too expensive to be used.

She was not included in the trade talks, although she listened hard to any conversation around her. When she'd mentioned her opinions on the second night to her new husband, he'd simply stared, then laughed and told her not to worry herself about men's business. She'd shrugged his amusement off, determined to prove her usefulness.

Nobody spoke to her during the day, unless it was Rylan asking if she needed anything. The guards and mule handlers stayed apart and Mekhi ignored her now she rode in the cart. The countryside made up for the deficiency in company. She'd never been this far from her home before. Her dreams were a tapestry of leaves and boughs, the sounds and smells intoxicating. She expressed her delight in the mountains, only to be chuckled at by the men. Feeling lost for the first time in her life, Mika became quieter as she realised anything she said would be discounted - her opinions didn't matter.

The mountains were huge, holding up the sky in the gaps between the trees. They were wild and rugged, taller than anything she'd ever seen. They formed a barrier around most of her country, there were only a couple of routes through, the sea blocked the rest. Spread out below them were the forests of Cassai, a swath of massive trees with lone sentinels bursting through to spread their branches in the sunlight. They were kept warm by the ocean currents, watered by the winds that were swept off the sea and cradled by the mountains.

The trail climbed, the trees became thinner, giving way to high pastureland. Dizzy from the wide views and height, she gazed down at her entire country, the sea pale in the distance that she'd never seen before. The mountain range that had guarded Cassai for hundreds of years from the rest of the world was treacherous, a maze of canyons and blind alleys. Cassai had never needed to patrol its backyard, until Ackbarr had discovered the way through. Even now few knew the complete way. A guide joined them at the last inn to take them through the passes. Rylan's mutter about the price he charged was quickly hushed by his father. He was a small stringy man with seamed skin and a tough little pony that trotted gamely upwards. He was the first non-Cassai Mika had seen apart from her new husband and his father and she wondered about the strangeness of being in a country full of dark haired people.

Homesickness beckoned as she lost sight of the last green tree. She swallowed back the tears, refusing to be seen as a weak woman. Her brother – she tried to stop herself, then stubbornly refused. Her brother would have been enjoying the adventure, talking eagerly with the guards, sharing everything. Mika had quickly realised her husband didn't even like her looking in the guard's direction. She snorted to herself, maybe he thought she might compare him to them. She was stuck on the cart, jolting in the stiff backed position of being a lady. She wondered what they would think if she stole a guard's horse and raced up the rocky trail, trusting in her horse's sure-footedness. Her blood pulsed in anticipation and she unconsciously sat straighter, unaware of the spark in her eyes and her husband's uneasy glance.

Rylan mistook her straightening, "We shan't reach the high pass for several days, you can't see it from here."

"How high do we go?" Desperate for any conversation, she leant towards him. Mika hoped she would have a chance to change her husband, to make him listen. He was still young, only a few years older than her. She held on tight to her promise, determined she'd become a good wife and rise to any occasion set in front of her.

"High enough for snow. You have seen snow?" The look on his face was patronizing.

She nodded and twitched away as he reached back into the cart to pull another cloak out for her. If she were riding astride, she'd have the horse's heat to warm her. Her eyes glazed, gazing upwards at the grey rocks.

The high pass took three days to get through. It was a rocky wasteland, a maze of valleys that all looked the same to her inexperienced eyes. Mekhi's complaining reached new heights as he was forced to sleep in a tent piled with blankets and braziers. Mika noticed how the guards pulled faces in his direction when he wasn't looking. Her cheeks flushed with cold under her tan, making her eyes sparkle. Snow was still on the mountain tops and she was grateful in some respects that she had an extra body in her blankets to keep her warm, even if it also meant she had someone else's hands on her.

The air felt stingingly alive, she puffed out fog with delight in the mornings. Mirroring his father, Rylan rose with reluctance and she had to stay in the tent until he got up. She lay with impatience, trying not to wriggle while he snored and listened to the men grumbling quietly outside. During the day, her eyes were everywhere, watching the rocks carefully from her cart, looking for signs of green, seeing tiny flowers tucked into the rocks and eagles riding in the currents high above.

The way down was steep, with a switchback trail. The guide had advised that she would be better off riding the pony and despite disliking the side saddle, Mika had agreed. The risks of the cart overturning on the narrow track were too high. She petted the pony absently, her mind lost in the clear air and peeping down at the mist coated valley spread out below them.

The trail widened and the views were amazing. Wrapped in her cloak, she kept her delight to herself and drank it in. The province of Fenin was the breadbasket of Ackbarr, large barns housed both grain and animals. The landscape was different here, not the tall forests she was used to, but rolling hills, patchworked with hedged fields and spotted with tiny specks of grazing cattle. It was dry and the large fields were golden in the late autumn, the mountains holding the rain on the Cassai side. It felt to her a soft country, tamed like her pony into giving what was needed. The houses she saw were larger, more open and richly decorated inside.

The meal at the inn fascinated her, the food reminding her that they'd left Cassai as sharply as the landscape outside. So much rich food, no wonder Mekhi was over-weight. She managed to embarrass Rylan by asking the innkeeper's wife about the pudding, a sweet pastry she'd never seen before. She couldn't believe the pastry could be rolled so thin, become so crispy, she'd thought it was vegetable based to begin with.

Mekhi waved her curiosity away with a disdainful laugh and for once, her enthusiasm overcame her resolve to behave. It was matched by the innkeeper's wife, who insisted on showing "the foreign girl" her kitchen. They spent half the evening together, with the wife delightedly showing Mika how the pastry was made, getting in her own cook's way as she did. Rylan told her off afterwards in their room for showing her ignorance in front of her inferiors. She didn't care, anything new fascinated her. She tried to remember everything, knowing Alma would be desperate to know and resolved to write as soon as she'd got to her new home.

Chapter 4

The outskirts of the city stank. Mika stared, appalled at the shacks leaning against each other, some barely standing. Children ran up to beg before being driven off by the guardsmen. She was handed some coins to give out. Mekhi and Rylan threw their offerings with disdain and she watched as the children scrabbled to catch them, barely dodging the horses. Mika clutched hers with indecision, who could she help? She caught first one child's eye, then another. Sores decorated their faces and stick thin limbs pleaded.

The tiny coins bit into her hand as the small faces stared at her. In a panic she scattered them, unused to beggars in her ordered world. The guardsmen pushed through, bellowing at the fingers touching the precious mules. She shrank away from the noisy implied violence, the imploring voices and the eyes staring at her. She pulled her stole over her head, trying to hide from them, vulnerable on the high seat of the cart.

A set of smartly dressed guards barred their way at the main gates, the beggars had dispersed to harass another traveller. Mika gazed at the huge walls, the stones neatly mortared, and then twisted to look over her shoulder at the mess behind. Those walls wouldn't protect the people living in the shacks. Mekhi was talking smoothly to the man in charge. No pomposity this time, they looked like old friends. Something changed hands while the regular guards stared ahead. A docket was issued, she presumed for taxes and they were let in.

Rylan rode next to her. "Is this Ackbarr?" she asked, thinking it was the capital city.

Her husband laughed, "No. Ackbarr is eight days travel from here. This is Fenin. It's a minor city in comparison, although still important for trade. We live in the north side with the rest of the merchants." The first time her husband had offered information.

Mika tried again, "Shall we go to Ackbarr?" That had been where her brother had shamed himself. She wondered if she could find out why if she went there.

Her husband replied pompously, "I shall. You will stay here and make my babies."

She swallowed her hurt and disappointment. Through blurring eyes she looked at the city. The roads were narrow, stalls set out made them tighter. Windows had flaps that came down to make booths. People shouting and yelling. Dogs and children running about, getting under their feet, barely dodging the horses. So many smells, both savoury and not. Latrines competed with bakeries. Bright colours of washing hanging from balconies, heaps of rubbish piled in alleyways. Open spaces, squares where fountains tinkled, people sitting, eating, talking. The cart thumped on the cobbles, jolting her tired back.

Mika pulled the edge of her stole further around her face to stop the stares. She was blonde compared to them. Those surrounding her had dark hair, blue eyes and tanned skin. She'd always thought her hair had been dark. Alma had often commented on the difference, twining their hair together to look in fascination at her own white blonde tresses and Mika's sandy strands. Here, Mika was the odd one out again.

They stopped outside a house in a small square with gated archways leading off. Large buildings surrounded the square, the grey walls several stories high. Shutters were on the lower floors and glass in the top stories only. Glass - a luxury. Everything looked well maintained, there were no beggars or urchins to disturb the peace. They waited, the riders milling around, while the mules were taken inside and offloaded quickly. Mekhi paid the leader, shaking his hand firmly with loud promises to contact him when they were needed again. The mules headed away in a different direction, she presumed to the stables.

The cart was driven through the archway which opened into a small yard. Mika was helped from the cart and stood, staring at her new home, wondering if she would be happy here. She took a deep breath, trying to stretch surreptitiously and was confronted by a plump woman only a few years older than herself. Rylan introduced her.

"Stepmother. This is Mika, my new bride." No introduction was coming from the other direction. Mika nodded and smiled in as friendly a fashion as she could. It wasn't returned. She was taller than the other woman and slimmer. Mika felt her anger returning as she was eyed up and dismissed. She hadn't asked to be here. She squashed the feeling, reminding herself of her good intentions, she was going to have to try harder.

The trader came over and enveloped his wife in ample arms. She must be his second wife, she wasn't old enough to be her husband's mother. Mika suppressed a wince at the way she cooed and fussed over Mekhi. She wondered how her new mother-in-law coped with the trader being in bed with her. Did he have to lift his paunch to find his prick? She stifled a giggle at the thought and stopped when she noticed the wife's hostile eyes on her.

They went through another gate into a tiny garden. A tinkling fountain, the plants carefully tended and seats sheltered under arbours. All the plants were clipped and weeded, it was very different from her mother's wildly twining vines. There was complete privacy from the noisy city under the high walls, life was muted here.

Mika was led up steps to the door onto the second floor. This led into the public area of the trader's house. The servants came to greet them, murmuring their delight at the trader being back. Everything was a riot of colour in the house, designed to show how important Mekhi was. The servants in comparison were quiet and discreet. Mika noticed none of them looked her in the eye, even when she tried. Disturbed, she allowed herself to be taken up to the next floor.

Their suite of rooms looked out over the street on one side. She ran over to touch the expensive glass gently and to look below at the people leaving the tiny square. Her husband smiled indulgently and showed her the rest of their rooms. To her delight there was a room to bathe in, with water coming out of a tap in the wall. Even in her father's house, the water had to be hauled in and heated. Here, the servants only had to bring the hot, the cold could be pumped up. Heavy carved furniture was pushed to the sides of the room. She started to unpack a bag that had been brought in and was stopped by Rylan.

"That's a servant's job. Your job is to please me."

She'd done nothing else since she'd married him. Sighing a little, she went to put her arms around him as he expected.

Afterwards, Mika lay in bed and tried not to see the servants unpacking her things as Rylan slept. She drummed her fingers under the covers and shifted him off her. He sighed and rolled over. The servants went about their business not looking in their direction, they'd come in halfway through Rylan's advances. He'd ignored them and carried on, not appearing to notice her embarrassment. The servants in her house had always knocked and waited, they were more like family. She tried to imagine this happening to her parents and failed.

Mika waited until they'd disappeared and slid out, wrapping something around herself in case they returned. To her delight, she found the bathtub full. She slid in, washing off the dust and sweat of travelling. Several slender glass vials were close by and she sniffed them, unsure whether to use them. She washed and dressed swiftly, not wanting to be found naked. Rubbing her hair dry as she walked into the next room, she gazed out of the window at the street, watching the square below with delight.

A grunt from Rylan in the bed, "You found the bath."

"Yes."

"Come here." She pulled the drapes against the possibility of servants coming in and let him pull her close. He nuzzled into her, enjoying the scent of clean skin, exciting himself.

That evening she struggled through a meal of rich food and listened to the trader boasting of his deals. Mika felt her new mother in law's eyes watching her and could tell she wasn't happy to have a rival in the house. Mika tried to be pleasant, remembering how her own mother behaved and felt the anger rising. It wasn't her fault, she was just another trade deal, only she was one that couldn't be sold on.

After dinner, sleepy from the travelling and heavy food, Mika watched Rylan struggling through the accounts set by his father. She listened to him complaining about the difficulty of the sums. She came to sit next to him and peered over his shoulder. He let her look through them, confident she'd be impressed by the columns and figures filling the page.

Mika worked her way through with growing delight. She could do this. Her brother had hated figures as well. She'd helped him too, maybe this was a way to help her new husband. She could do them for him. She imagined them being able to work together, talking about their business when he was older, sitting by the fireside and working through the day. In her enthusiasm, she pointed out several mistakes, meaning to show him the how and why.

Rylan stared at her. "How do you know this?"

"I used to help my brother. Look it's easy, you just missed the..."

He gathered the papers together, eyebrows lowered. "I will do it. It is not a fit occupation for a woman."

Exasperated, she snapped back, "Nothing is a fit occupation for a woman. I've done nothing since I've been with you. I can help you. If you don't want your father to know, that's fine."

His face showed confusion and then firmed into stubbornness, "Your job is to have my babies. It's important. Nothing should distract you from that. Are you growing one yet?"

"I don't know. A few figures won't make any difference. I'm bored, let me help you."

"Babies. That is your job. Concentrate on it."

He sniffed and walked out. Mika slumped on the bench. Babies. She was barely fifteen. Was she pregnant yet? Would he let her help him after she'd had a baby? She imagined herself pregnant. Fat and waddling as she'd seen other women. The walls started to close in around her.

Unable to breathe she went and stared out of the window. A rhythmic thumping started from the suite of rooms next door. A voice crying out. It was her new mother-in-law and the trader. She could hear the falseness in the cries and wondered if he was taken in by it or maybe he didn't care.

Rylan went with his father to a nearby town, to learn about processing techniques in the weeks after their arrival. They went out during the evening, sometimes taking Mika and her mother-in-law with them. She learnt after a few occasions that Mekhi preferred her to keep her hair covered. People knew Rylan had married a foreign girl, they just didn't want to be reminded.

Her mother-in-law, Ardi, had her own group of friends. Conversations spluttered to a halt after the first few pleasantries. Feeling uncomfortable with them, Mika sampled the food provided and it gave her a way in on the conversations with the other guests, asking questions they were pleased to answer. She silently thanked the innkeeper's wife for the evening they'd spent talking about food. Mika listened more than she spoke. She had to admit that behind the boasting, Mekhi did know a lot about his trade. There was a shrewd knowledge behind his pomposity and he had an eye to what would sell.

During the day she was stuck in the house with her mother-in-law. No chance of going out, Ardi had expressed horror at the thought of Mika wandering the streets. She was told a lady only visited friends. Mika heard the implied meaning that she didn't know anyone and she wasn't worth visiting. Mika resolved to try and at least make one acquaintance the next time she was taken out by Rylan.

Ardi went out almost every day, gossiping with her friends. On the occasions they came to her house, they made no pretence of welcome when Mekhi or Rylan weren't around. They stopped talking and stared at her when she came into the room. Eventually she stopped trying to be friendly and simply kept a pretence of civility up.

Bored, Mika tried making friends with the servants. Back home, the servants and guards had been part of the family. She was frustrated to find she had to corner the servants to get them to talk about anything that wasn't an order. Mumbled replies and worried looks were most of what she got. Eventually the steward gently took her aside and explained she was distracting them from their duties.

She snuck into the library several times, thinking she could learn about her new culture by reading. At least, Mekhi called it his library, it was a shelf of books in a room of tapestries. The books were mostly about fabrics. She read, uninspired, thinking that at least she could talk to her husband with some knowledge, until the day a servant found her looking. He was so upset that she left and didn't return.

Mika wondered how her family was, whether her father had left home to resume his duties in Ackbarr and if he would visit her here. Her mother would be in her garden, her brother and sisters playing. Alma would be missing her, when they weren't staying at each other's houses, they would write constantly. She could think of pages to write, most of it about her boredom and yet more about Rylan's wants. That raised a smile as she paced the room, she imagined Alma's wide eyes, the exclamations from her and the confidences they could share. She daren't ask for pen and paper, admitting she could do sums better than Rylan was bad enough, but she also knew her handwriting was clearer.

She wandered the small garden and watched the square outside. Life was passing her by. She longed to be stretching her legs, riding and laughing, mocking the other boys in her brother's presence. Itchy all over with restlessness, Mika brooded over her brother's disappearance, the swiftness of her wedding and her mother's upset. Her normal personality had asserted itself since the shock of her marriage, she struggled to contain it and wondered why bother if she would be here forever.

Rylan left to help his father on another trip. Mika suspected it was more listening than helping, but nodded her head as he'd proudly told her. He'd mentioned before leaving that she needed to start making the clothes for all the babies he intended her to have. She delightedly asked Ardi for the fabrics and threads, something she couldn't be refused, seeing as it was a fitting occupation for her status. Her pleasure was short lived, she quickly remembered she hated sewing and it made her back and fingers ache. Reluctantly she started, anything to stop the boredom.

Mika lived for her dreams at night. Stalking through the forest, alive. She thought through them during the day while sewing. Remembering her journey, she added details – colours and smells, until it felt more real than her waking life. There were times when she jumped as a servant walked into the room, having forgotten where she was.

Delighted to have anything different happening, she greeted Rylan with enthusiasm when he came back. Even his clumsy claiming of her body couldn't dampen it. His first question afterwards was whether she was pregnant or not. She shrugged. Could be, it was too early to tell. The thought of having something of her own had started to appeal to her.

Walking past Mekhi's study that evening, she heard voices. She stopped in the hall, not intending to listen. It was Ardi, complaining about something.

"… constantly trying to talk to the servants, distracting them. They'll be thinking they're as good as us shortly."

Mika heard him rumble soothingly, "She's a foreigner, give her a chance. They have different customs there. She'll learn."

"One of them found her in your library, goodness knows what she was doing." Mika could almost see Ardi waving her hands helplessly.

"That's easily sorted. I can lock the door and give you the key."

An anger began to rise, as she heard Ardi saying, "I can't control her. She's surly with me, I've tried my best..." The tone implied Ardi couldn't do anything. She'd heard similar things when Ardi had her friends around. Her friends assuring Ardi that it was a dreadful thing to have a daughter in law that didn't appreciate her.

"Come here..." She heard the trader's voice deepen as the chair creaked under his weight and Ardi's soft laugh.

Mika crept away, not wanting to hear any more. She thought hard, had she been difficult? It was hard fitting in, it was a very different culture, but Ardi hadn't tried to help either. She tried to look from Ardi's perspective and failed, she wasn't used to this, preferring to act rather than think.

She pleaded for an allowance from Rylan. Taking her cue from Ardi, Mika had learnt to ask for favours quietly, with her eyes down and it pleased him to grant them. Hiding her distaste at having to ask in this way, she'd suggested it would be nice for her to choose the fabrics and skeins of thread for baby clothes. She showed him the clothes she'd made, pointing out they were too stiff for a baby's soft skin. She'd twisted the idea, to include sewing for herself. Rylan agreed, he liked the idea of her sitting quietly doing domestic tasks.

Delighted at the chance to get out of the house, she picked a servant and agreed to take a guard with her. Ardi watched, stone faced as she left and Mika struggled to stop herself grinning. The cold winter rain lashed down, she wore her Cassai boots and held her skirts scandalously high to avoid them getting soaked. Even not being allowed to haggle with the stall holders failed to dampen her delight. A servant would do that for her, as a lady she was expected to point and allow him to do the hard work. The noise, being amongst other people, the smells and shoving intoxicated her.

She bought a tiny amount of fabric, pretending to be overwhelmed by the choice. In reality it gave her another excuse to get out of the house. Mika talked to the servants accompanying her, treating them with the little money she had. They opened up warily as she curried their favours. Carefully while looking for the fabrics she needed, she explored the city, gazing at the big buildings, the temples and the curtain walls surrounding the city. Everything was so different from her home country. She could see why they thought Cassai was backwards. Cassai was based on small towns and compounds, the buildings tucked into the forest with large trees shading the streets. The Cassai population wasn't big enough to support a city this size. They didn't have statues of people either, most were of animals or stylised renderings of the trees and plants.

Everywhere there was talk of Ackbarr, how Cassai was defying it over the exporting of the timber needed for warships. Mika felt a surge of pride, their trees were the best, tall straight hardwood that would last. Their craftspeople were the best at making the long lean ships that cut through the waters. In theory Cassai was a duchy of Ackbarr, but one allowed to rule itself, another thorn in the side for the people of Fenin. But Cassai had never been truly conquered, it still had its royal family and its own way of governing. She caught people's startled glances when they noticed her features and accent. The talk around her would go quiet for a moment, then hurriedly start again.

She asked the servants questions about the buildings and statues that they could rarely answer. It frustrated her when they shrugged away their indifference to the sights around them. She couldn't ask her husband, they'd moved beyond the market at that point. The servants didn't care where she went and would stay quiet. While they followed her, they didn't have to work.

Rylan went on another trip with his father, leaving her with Ardi. The explorations and the money were stopped despite her protests. The servants looked apologetic when she tried to go out, barring her way. Ardi smirked and flounced off to see her friends.

Chapter 5

Mika heard a clatter in the courtyard and ran to the window. It had been another month. Rylan was in the bath, Mekhi downstairs. They weren't due to leave for a few days, so it couldn't be the mule train. Stocky horses milled down below, built for endurance rather than speed. Her breath caught as she spotted a flash of pale hair when someone pulled down a hood - Cassai. Her father, the passes must be finally open from the winter snow.

She almost flew down the stairs to meet him and then caught herself. She wanted to run into his arms, feel his familiar embrace, height and smell. Wail into his shoulder that she was unhappy and missed everyone. She felt her stomach tighten. She couldn't, she was married and they would be watching her. She stopped, tears prickling behind shut eyes and felt sick. Mika wondered if her mother had ever felt like this, unable to do as she wanted.

There was a noise from the bathroom, Rylan had heard the commotion and wandered out naked. She averted her eyes, still not used to his lack of inhibition.

"Who is it?"

"My father." Her voice was curiously flat in her ears. He nodded and got dressed, walked down with her.

She gave her father a subdued greeting, inhibited by everyone watching. All through the midday meal Mika was tense. Her father made polite conversation with both Mekhi and Rylan, charming Ardi into giggles. Mika felt sick watching her and tried to hide it as she saw her father notice.

After the meal her father begged their forgiveness and asked for a few minutes with her alone. They were left in the dining room, her father requested the servants leave them and shut the door. He was at ease with ordering them around she noticed.

"You will be staying tonight?" Her formality belied her need to have him stay.

He shook his head, "I cannot. I need to be in Ackbarr and I made a detour to get here." He shrugged, "Business. Are you happy?" He'd caught her out, she couldn't reply, simply looked away. He leant against a table, "It's not easy, trying to assimilate into a different culture."

She glanced over her shoulder at the shut door, "It's killing me Papa." She'd not used that word in years, it all burst out in a strained whisper. "I can't do anything here."

He held out his arms and she finally flung herself into them sobbing. He let her cry for a while and then peeled her off, wiping her tears away. "It would have been difficult in any marriage for you, even if you had married within our country. You've had far greater freedoms than most girls even dream of."

"Do you keep Mother captive?"

Her father looked startled, "Can you imagine me doing that?" Mika blinked and thought, for all her soft words, her mother ruled the house. The amount of time her father was away, she had to. He continued firmly, "Your mother chooses to stay where she is, no more. I would not keep her against her will. We had arranged for your brother to marry in Fenin as well, you would not have been so alone..." He trailed off and stared at the wall. His face was set in the neutral mask which meant he was concealing strong feelings.

He touched her face. "Prove to me that you are my daughter. You must learn how to deal with the differences, accept what you can't change and work to change the things you can." She nodded, her vague dream of sneaking away with him shredded. "I have a few things in my saddlebags for you, including letters."

Mika brightened, a letter from her mother? A knock on the door interrupted them and a quiet voice saying they had to leave. She wiped her eyes and tucked her arm into his as they walked out to the courtyard. Mekhi spoke a few words while Ardi steamed in the background. Her father winked at Mika as he kissed her cheek, handing her a large parcel. She clutched it.

"I will drop in again on my way back." This was addressed to Mekhi, who nodded, looking important as though it were he who her father wanted to see.

Mika pulled herself together to wave him out the archway, ignoring Ardi's hissed whispers to Mekhi. She pleaded to go upstairs to their rooms to open her parcel in privacy.

Upstairs she jealously took her time, opening the parcel slowly. A scarf, embroidered clumsily by her little sisters was wrapped around everything, a small wood carving from her little brother, several letters and a couple of books. She opened the larger of the two carefully, it was one of her favourites. The folk tales of her country, the stylized prints of animals and plants every few pages were as important as the text in telling the story. She ran her fingers down the pages lovingly as the door opened and Rylan came in.

"What's that?"

"My father gave me a copy of my favourite book. Look, it's beautiful."

Rylan frowned, "You shouldn't have that."

"Why not? It's in Cassai, I could read the tales to you. You might enjoy them."

"You can read?"

"Yes in both your language and mine."

He looked uncertain, "I shouldn't let you have it. People will talk if they see you with it."

Inspiration hit her, "We could say it's yours. A present from my father and that you are reading it to find out more about our culture. It might help if you are dealing with my people in the future, you never know what information might help."

His face tightened and he said stiffly, "I can't read your language."

"I could teach you." She wheedled, desperate not to have him take the book away. "I've learnt so much from you over the last months. These are only folk tales, but a Cassai trader would give you more respect if you knew what he meant when he talked about the mouse in the grain house for instance. It would impress your father too."

Greed won him over, he nodded and Mika tried not to show her relief. She wondered if this was how her father felt, negotiating as an ambassador of a small country. Ackbarr could choose to invade her country at any point. She'd realised over the last few months of listening that it was simply not worth it at the moment. She'd been sheltered, despite her father's status or perhaps because of it. He wouldn't have wanted her to know that he might be in danger.

Mika set the book on their table that evening, she copied out the letters for Rylan and showed him how to sound out the phonetic Cassai language. They spent the evening pouring over the book with Mika trying to control her impatience with his slowness. They laughed over the story of the lascivious little bat and the lamp in the moon. The bat trying to see into the lady's dressing room, flitting and twirling while she changed her dresses. The lady teasing the bat, sometimes leaving her light on and sometimes pulling the drapes to shut the moon out.

They began to spend every evening together after he'd done his work for his father. Rylan still wouldn't let her see the sums he struggled with but he started to talk about his day and she asked him questions, making her suggestions as innocently as possible. She had to stop herself from dancing with delight when he mentioned doing something that she'd suggested and how it had worked. She began to feel more content, her dreams of the forest more a habit rather than a necessity and she would curl up to listen to Rylan instead of pacing impatiently.

Mika showed him how to read the pictures he'd scoffed at and how they tied in with the story. She deliberately stumbled over the words, making him feel better about his slow progress and lied, telling him that she knew the stories by rote, that reading them was far harder.

Realisation hit him one evening, as she smothered a tired yawn. "I've seen this picture before, on a building in Dunbarin."

"We have them carved into the walls of our buildings, children learn from them. Adults are reminded of the stories."

"So, every picture is a story?"

"Yes."

"I thought they were just pictures." His own face was a picture as he realised what he'd been missing.

She tried not to smile, she remembered her father saying how foreigners missed so much about their culture. "Any Cassai will be delighted to tell you the story if you ask. Especially if you can figure some of it out for yourself. Have you seen the carving on the temple walls?"

He nodded, "All the birds in the trees."

"It talks about the devotion the birds show to the sun every day when it rises. Look, here's the story, see the same picture?"

They talked on, Mika trying to show him how a Cassai thought. Rylan was faster than she thought he would be at times. He did look at the world around him, but dismissed much of it, absorbed in his own superiority. He was very much like her brother in that respect.

The conversation had changed to Cassai later that week when Mekhi had several fellow merchants at their house. Ardi and Mika had been invited to entertain the wives. One of the merchants had become drunk and made a rude comment. To Mika's surprise Rylan spoke up, defending her country. Mekhi blinked at his son's views and Rylan having caught the look, stumbled in his explanation.

Mika dared to comment, "My father gave Rylan a book on our culture." Mekhi's gaze swung to her in surprise at her speaking up. "My father said you can never learn too much about a different country. Rylan's taught me so much."

It felt to her that she was laying it on too thick. Mekhi merely nodded his agreement, muttered something to his colleague about his foreign daughter in law and changed the subject. Rylan gazed at her with more respect. Ardi scowled at her plate as Mika smiled back at Rylan.

The letters she took her time reading and re-reading, carefully smoothing them down each time. One from her mother, one from Alma, a few words from her siblings. She stole a single sheet of paper from Rylan's workbook, trying to figure out what she could and couldn't write down. Things were better between her and Rylan. She was in a quandary over her writing, she wasn't supposed to be able to write well. She decided to write anyway and give the letter to her father when she saw him next. In keeping with his advice, she decided to write only positive comments, then promptly ran out of ideas after describing her journey.

Her mother had included several sachets of her favourite vineflower, dried and then stitched into little pockets. Her mother would often slip one under both Kaylan and her pillow for sweet dreams. There was always some drying in the house, holding onto its scent for months at a time. Mika tucked them into her clothes. Rylan flinched when Mika showed it to him and she laughed, pressing them to her own nose and inhaling the odd peppery citrus smell with delight.

Mika was curled up in a chair one evening, vaguely wishing her period would hurry up. She was fed up, feeling tired and grumpy. Her stomach had been blown up for the last few weeks, feeling tight and uncomfortable. Rylan had made a comment about the amount of food she'd pinched off his evening snack plate when the look on her face stopped him.

"What is it?"

Mika had started counting and bit back a word Kaylan had taught her and she knew Rylan wouldn't approve of. "My period's late."

He started to recoil at something he didn't want to know, then realised that maybe he did. "You mean..." A smile started to spread over his face.

"Maybe, it's too early to tell."

He was delighted, "We need to tell father." Mika wasn't sure how she felt, she certainly didn't want Ardi knowing yet. She looked around the room, suffocating, wishing she was back home and realised with horror that she would never go home again. Nearly in tears, she pleaded for him to wait, suggesting it would be a lovely surprise for his father when they came back. Rylan continued to fuss over her throughout the evening, constantly stopping his reading to look at her with pride.

On the morning Rylan was due to go away, Mika woke before he did. She lay for a moment, wondering why she'd woken when a horrendous feeling crept over her. A sleepy grunt was all she had from Rylan as she rushed to the privy retching. Nothing came up and she staggered back to their bed where he lay, still half asleep and blinking.

"What's the matter?"

"I nearly threw up." She was in no mood to reassure him.

"Should we get a Medici in? Are you ill?" He began scrabbling for his bedclothes.

Mika curled up, feeling weak and not wanting to talk. "I think we can agree that I'm pregnant. It's something my mother told me about."

He grinned, trying to hug her clumsily while she lay there wanting to die. A knock on the door indicated a servant coming in to remind Rylan to get up. A breakfast tray was in his hands. One smell set Mika running to the privy again to Rylan's delighted laughter.

Rylan actually looked sad to leave, showing his concern for her as he said his goodbyes down in the yard. Ardi's slitted eyes behind the trader's back showed she'd noticed the change in his attitude. Mika watched him go with the lighter feeling that she was starting to make a difference.

The mornings continued with her retching. Mika tried to eat in small quantities. Ardi's sniping grew worse than ever, she'd quickly worked out Mika's condition. She didn't miss her walks outside this time, she curled up in their rooms and looked at the books her father had given her. When she picked up the other one, she discovered it was a book of love poems. Mika flushed when she read through them, wondering what Rylan would think.

Mika could vaguely remember her mother's last pregnancy. The knowledge of being pregnant was very different to wishing. She was feeling vulnerable, her body changing, aching in odd places. She wished her mother were with her, but she couldn't get any word to her. No way would Ardi allow her to send a letter. She comforted herself with the thought that she could tell her father when he next came.

Rylan had been gone for weeks, she missed their sessions with the books, the light in his eyes when he got something right. Her stomach had been feeling unsettled all day. During supper time Mika felt a cramp twisting her insides. She wanted to lie down and curl up in bed. Ardi narrowed her eyes and in her most spiteful mood, refused to allow her to leave. Mika waited patiently through the long meal while her stomach complained further. At the first opportunity she escaped to her rooms.

On going to the privy she discovered a few drops of blood on her dress. Her breath caught, this shouldn't be happening – was this normal? She had no idea. Mika changed and the spasms got worse. The second time she went to the privy there were more stains. She walked slowly around their rooms, stretching as she tried to ease the cramps and failed. Worry tightened her stomach further.

Finally, wiping the tears from her face and not knowing what else to do, she went to Ardi. "I'm bleeding."

Ardi continued flicking through her sewing basket, her face turned away, "And? It happens."

"Shouldn't we call someone?"

"Nothing anyone can do." Ardi's voice plainly said she would do nothing. Mika had to get back to the privy and she sat there despairing at the blood. Tears rose, she wanted her mother, anyone to help her and she had no one.

She dealt with that night alone. The servants stayed away as she sat upright, unable to lie down comfortably. Finding rags that soaked through so quickly, wondering how much blood she could lose and if she would die. The pain, the long hours staring at the walls, the unreal feeling in the small circle of candlelight. The urgent rushing to the privy, the waiting and the sense of losing something she'd never really acknowledged.

Morning finally came through the shutters, the slabs of light hitting her bleary eyes. Mika was too exhausted to cry as she discovered she was finally able to lie down on their bed. She slept, dreamless.

The servants crept around her that day, unsure what to do. She ignored them, staring at the wall, her eyes swollen. She'd miscarried her baby. Now she'd lost it, she wanted it back badly. Tucked up safe inside her. Only it hadn't been, her body hadn't wanted it enough. She went through everything she'd done, wondered about every action. She had no one to talk to, she would have even been grateful for any crumbs of sympathy from Ardi.

Ardi remained separate from her. Mika wandered her rooms listlessly, waiting for Rylan to come home. With little exercise, she ate and slept badly. Ardi spitefully refused to let her eat in her rooms and food was only served at the table while the menfolk weren't there. Mika had the choice of sitting with Ardi smirking at her or not eating. More often than not, Mika chose to go hungry. She developed dark circles under her eyes, losing weight. Weeks passed and her body healed. She remained upset, worrying over how Rylan would react.

A noise outside disturbed her and she peered through the window into the courtyard. It was Rylan, she saw him dismount and Ardi go to him. She hunched away from the window. It was chaos out there, mules being unloaded, the cart at an angle. The shouting and calling came drifting up. She curled back up on the bed, the pain returning, sick at the thought of having to tell him.

A noise on the stairs, the door opened and he came in. Tears came into her eyes, she sat up and reached out her hand, "I lost it."

"I heard." His voice was flat.

She felt pressure building up inside, "I wanted..."

"Stepmother told me." Mika stared, what had Ardi told him? "You've been looking at father's library," He strode over and swept her books off the chest, kicked at them. "You've been going to places outside the market, lying to me about where you went. The servants have said you ordered them to take you. You probably caught something." He was vibrating with anger.

"I'm sorry. I was bored, I didn't mean..."

"You killed my baby."

She gaped. His baby? It wasn't his. He'd not been the one carrying it, he'd not spent the night losing it and the weeks crying and grieving. Something twisted inside, why did she bother? He didn't care about her. Her voice came out thin and shrill, "It was my baby, not yours. I wanted it. I asked Ardi for a Medici, she wouldn't help."

His face set into an expression she'd not seen before and something caught her hard on the side of her head. She stumbled and without thought she swung back, fighting him in a way she never had before, all her frustrations coming out at once. His outrage increased as he finally managed to pin her to the bed. She was hissing and spitting, he had nail marks down his face.

"You are a hellcat. I should have known better than to listen to you. I have been told that a woman is more fertile straight after losing a baby. You will be pregnant again and this time you will keep it." Mika saw Ardi's smirk behind the statement, he wouldn't know such a thing.

He held her down and she was shocked by his strength. Exhausted by the miscarriage and the weeks of not eating properly she could only fight him so far.

Rougher than he had ever been, he left her on the bed, crying through helplessness and outrage.

Mika wrapped herself up in her sheets, hiding in the fragile security for a long time. Rylan had bathed and left the rooms without saying another word to her. She was aware of the distant tinkle of Ardi's laugh and the murmurs as the guests came for dinner in the quiet of the upstairs rooms. The servant stood helplessly in the doorway when she ignored him asking her to come down and he left, not returning.

Eventually she pulled herself up, and wincing at the bruises, slowly cleaned herself. Her thoughts whirled around as she changed into her night clothes, how couldn't he see what she'd lost? Why was he so blind? She'd looked to him for a measure of comfort, denied to her from everyone else and he'd believed his step mother. Everything they'd done together over the last few months had been lost.

She desperately sought sanctuary in her dreams, tried to bring them to her. She could only stare at the wall and the patterns in the plasterwork. Her mouth was dry and she ignored it, caught up in her misery. Rylan came up later and lay next to her, bleary with wine. Mika tensed, wondering if he would try to touch her again. He seemed to take ages to settle down, snuffling and moving around in bed. She pretended to be asleep and eventually his breathing turned into a light snore that kept her awake further.

Staring at the ceiling, she watched the moons glow through the slats of the shutters, moving slowly across the room. The light changed in her tired eyes, morphing into the flickering of moonlight through leaves at the edge of the forest. She paced through the undergrowth, her Mika-self only a dream of being trapped elsewhere. Her upset and frustration coiled tight, pushing her down a tunnel. Dreams of the night she'd lost the baby turned into dreams of blood, channelling her upset into anger. They'd forced her into a mould she couldn't cope with, chained her, caged her. She dreamt of lashing out, of hunger, her mouth filled with blood, claws catching flesh, rending it, red flesh tearing and exultant.

Chapter 6

Mika woke, feeling strangely tired and stretched, her muscles aching. Warmth suffused her, it was early morning, no one would be up yet. She stopped her stretch remembering last night. Her thoughts turned dark and she wondered what would happen this morning. The weak sunlight filtered through the slats and turned the pillow red.

She rolled over, still half asleep and stopped. The pillows were cream. She looked back at the pillow and along. Rylan was lying next to her, eyes open, staring upwards. His throat had been ripped out, the tattered flesh shaking from the movement of the bed, mimicking life. She stared, stupid in shock, seeing how the blood had dried in detail, the splattered wall and how his mouth was hanging open idiotically. Last night she'd wanted him dead, had no longer cared, had wanted to get away from him, this morning...

Her gaze widened, there was blood everywhere, on her. Her hands were coated in it. They came up to her mouth as she smothered her screams. Took them away as she tasted the iron. Whimpering, she wondered how she'd slept through this, why she'd not been killed as well. Her face felt strange. She pulled the covers back and tottered to the mirror he'd been so proud of. The smeary reflection looked back at her. Her face was masked with blood, her hair stringy with it.

Looking at the floor she could see half a bloody print leading to the door. She went cold, it wasn't hers, it wasn't even human. Without thinking, she knelt to measure it with her hand. The palm of her hand only just covered the print. Some kind of animal, how had it got in here? Why had she been spared? She vaguely blamed Ardi, had she let a dog in here? Did she dislike Rylan that much? Ardi had always been nice to him, to the point where Mika had wondered if she'd had designs on marrying him after the trader had died.

In her panic the only thing Mika could think of was that she had to get away. She knew she'd be blamed for this. Ardi had blamed her often enough for things, loudly and in public. They wouldn't believe her, they held her people in contempt. Mika hurriedly scrubbed the blood away, it even coated the soles of her feet. Washing was hard in the cold water ad she dared not summon a servant for hot.

Creeping around, trying not to look at the bed, she considered her options. As a woman she wasn't safe, she could barely move in the clothes she wore. She'd seen other women outside, they were always escorted by a man. She didn't know any men, she didn't have anyone. Mika stopped herself, but what if she were dressed as a man? Her hands went up to her mouth at her audacity, she was a married woman. With that thought her eyes were dragged back to the bed – she wasn't married anymore.

Mika forced herself to breathe, if she cut off her hair she could pass. She knew her height and slim build would work for her and people had often assumed she'd been a male twin to her brother when her hair had been hidden.

Decision made, she went through her husband's clothes, finding those that were old, simple and not too big. Her hands shook as she fumbled with haste, she had to get away before anyone woke. Again, her height helped, while she had to wear a belt, nothing was too long for her. She re-tied her corset to flatten rather than emphasise her breasts, feeling grateful that they were small. Coming across one of the sachets her mother had made from the vineflowers, she pressed it to her face and then tucked it into her pocket, desperately needing a reminder of home.

She pulled her hair into a tail at the back of her head and cut it with her husband's dagger. Her husband - she tried not to think of the mess left on the bed. Letting her hair fall around her face, she stared, confronted by her brother in the mirror, then stuffed her cut hair down the privy. She'd still have to disguise her hair, although dark for her country, she was still far too blonde for Fenin and she couldn't wear a hood all the time. Frantically thinking, she remembered Mekhi had some dye in his rooms. Ardi would dye his hair, he was going grey and didn't like it. She would fuss over him, fawning and coyly teasing in the simpering tones he liked.

Rylan had left the door jammed open from last night, not bothering to close it in his stupor. Mika slipped through, avoiding the paw prints and crept out on to the landing. She went cold. The paw prints led to Mekhi's rooms. Had it really been Ardi?

Their door was ajar, she listened carefully, her ear pressed against the door, trying to hear any a large animal that might still be around. Carefully she pushed it open, tense in the expectation that she'd have to pull it shut quickly. Peering around she found blood everywhere here as well. Mika caught a sight of a soaked bed, the pillows and sheets torn, a mess on the bed and another on the floor. She tried not to look at the white bones gleaming as she ran into the room. No sound, the same deathly silence as she snatched the packet she'd come for. She ran out and into the corridor and slammed the door shut, retching dryly.

Worse than she'd thought. All of them dead. She felt very alone in the big house. The stillness seemed to accuse her. She hadn't done anything! There was no one else alive, someone must have brought the animal in. Mekhi made sharp deals, she'd seen that, but he'd always left his rivals with something, no one had hated him this much that she knew of. She tried to think if the servants would do something like this and shook her head, all she could think of was that she had to get away.

Shivering, she tiptoed down the stairs to the main rooms and took some money from Mekhi's drawer in his study. The servants had their own place on the bottom floor, the top was locked away from them. For once she was pleased that they were kept separate. The steward had a key, they all knew the trader slept in late most mornings – his deals were done late at night while drinking. She took the key from the alcove and locked the door to the courtyard steps behind her.

The morning was fresh, the city just waking up. The horses snuffled in the small stable kept in the courtyard. Mekhi wouldn't walk anywhere if he could ride. She longed for the companionship of another living being, even a horse. She shook her head, she'd be more obvious if she rode. People would notice a horse with a boy on it, they'd ask questions and it would cost to feed it.

Still feeling too conspicuous, Mika pulled the hood of the cloak over her head, hiding her blonde hair. She wandered the streets, with no idea of where she was going. Her stomach rumbled, a normality in the nightmare she was living. She bought bread from the bakeries opening for the workers and ducked her head away from the baker's enquiring look.

The panic rose again, she had to get out of here, she was too different, she'd get caught and they hated Cassai here. Fenin laws were harsh, she'd heard the men talking about this or that happening and the punishments given. They'd always lowered their voices when they'd noticed her listening but she'd heard enough. Remembering the way to the curtain wall was hard, it had been months since she'd been allowed out. Getting lost more than once, she pretended she was a boy looking for items for her master and asked several tradesmen who pointed her in the right direction.

The gate was just opening when she got there. There was a queue of people waiting, she joined them and kept her head down. In the rush of wagons coming in and out, she slipped through without notice and walked hurriedly away.

Mika slowed, panting with exertion and having done more exercise than she was used to. Her eye was caught by the small stone buildings on the both sides of the road. She wondered what they were for. A statue of a woman weeping caught her eye. She wondered if it was a shrine to a goddess, she'd not seen any female statues before. The emotion caught her, echoing how she felt as curiosity penetrated her dullness. She touched the inscription and whispered a prayer before bending to read it. "For my beloved Andres. Taken too soon." She walked to the next one, a similar inscription and realised it was a grave marker. They were all graves. Cassai bodies were burned, the ashes scattered in the small fields. She gazed about, amazed they had so much land to spare simply for burying people, how far did the graveyard stretch?

She remembered the bodies left in the house and hurried on, wanting to be as far away from the city as she could before they were discovered. A slum started at the end of the graveyard, tiny shacks, not much bigger than the tombs. This time, absorbed in her own troubles she didn't notice the children and dogs roaming and apart from a few catcalls, she too was ignored.

Mika stopped as the slums abruptly came to an end. A filthy stream trickled past, the banks were coated with effluent from the city and figures of children played in it further down. She jumped as a cart driver yelled at her to move out of the way. Mika pulled over, gazing at the road and the hills beyond. She didn't know which gate she'd gone through or where she was heading. She turned to look, the jagged mountains to Cassai were on the other side of the city. The range twisted further into the distance and marched across the horizon to face her. They were less high, but further away. She still had no way of getting over them. Not enough food or money. She shrugged and trudged along the road without a choice.

The sun came up as she walked, making her hot in the cloak. Pulling it off, she remembered her hair and the dye in her bag. She found a stream and used a strip torn from her cloak to dab it onto her hair, trying not to get it on her skin. It was certainly darker, but she wasn't entirely sure how successful she'd been, it was impossible to see her reflection clearly in the stream.

Sheep were scattered on the hilly fields and small farms in the wide valleys with managed copses topping the hills. She met other travellers on the road and to her relief she was ignored. She walked, on edge, always worried there might be a thundering of hooves behind her, shouts and the sound of dogs on her trail. Aware she didn't have much food, she ate lightly, unwilling to expose herself by buying more. She drank from streams away from the road. The afternoon rolled towards sunset. She plodded on, wary at every cart and rider that went by, expecting someone to identify her.

Mika decided to stop in a small wood before it got too dark. Her stomach grumbled and she was weary from not eating properly since the miscarriage. She cut another strip from her cloak, made a noose and hung it by a rabbit trail, hoping to catch one. Her brother and she'd caught and cooked rabbits before. Her brother… tears came finally. What had happened? How come she'd been spared? Those paw prints on the floor, even her feet had been covered in blood. She screwed up her eyes, trying to remove the memory of Rylan lying next to her.

Mika's hands shook as she remembered – she'd put on a clean nightdress that evening and had been naked when she'd woken up. There'd been rags on the bed, red and sodden. Nothing could have taken her nightdress off without her waking. Torn flesh flickered in front of her eyes and for a mad moment she wondered if it could have been her.

She whimpered, curling up in a ball, the roots of the tree digging into her side. Looking at her slender fingers she scrubbed clean, she curled them up into the sleeves of her shirt. She could never have ripped anything like that, she wasn't strong enough. Either of the two men could have held her off easily. People would have heard, especially if they were yelling but it didn't look like either of them had the chance. A vague glimmer of a struggle, hands pushing at her, the taste…

Mika's stomach heaved at the thread of memory and the thrill that ran through her.

Mika scrubbed her face and stood. She couldn't deal with all the wondering, all the possibilities. She had to deal with what was now, she'd go mad otherwise. She needed food and somewhere to sleep, a fire. She rummaged through her pockets and found nothing and closed her eyes in despair - she had no way of starting a fire. Mekhi or Rylan had never had to start a fire, they had people to do those things for them. She looked at the sky and took a deep breath telling herself that the spring night was fine and warm. She had no problems with sleeping outside, she had a thick cloak to wrap herself up in. Her brother would have had problems recognising his sister at that point, none of the spark and bounce left, she only a shaky determination to survive.

She went back to check the trap and found nothing in it, just as well as she had nothing to cook it on and didn't think she could deal with killing anything. She tucked the strip back in her bag and ate some of the bread instead.

Tears welled as she thought of her baby and Rylan's reaction. She didn't know the enough about the laws in this land. Would they try to take her back to Fenin or would they just hang her by the side of the road for the death of her husband? She felt her face carefully, maybe she could say she'd been an apprentice and that her master had beaten her. Would that be enough? Her fingers met nothing and prodded further, there were no bruises. Rylan had hit her hard enough to bruise and she now couldn't feel them. Unable to think, she curled up and exhausted from the day's walking, she fell asleep immediately.

She woke early, just before dawn. Despite her worries, her night had been dream free. The birds were deafening in the trees and everything was misty. She moved to brush her hair out of her eyes and remembered the previous day as her fingers trailed through air. It was chilly in the pre-dawn, she sat and watched as the sun came over the horizon, flooding the countryside with colour. Mika caught a movement below her on the road and stared with mild curiosity. It was horsemen galloping. She wondered what they were doing and then realised the bodies would have been discovered. They would want her back to face justice. They wouldn't believe her, she was a foreigner. No one would help her.

Where could she go? Not home, that was the first place they'd look, on the road to the Cassai mountains. Her face sagged into her knees and she forced herself to think through the desperation of wanting her mother. She needed to hide, somewhere with people. She remembered Rylan telling her of Ackbarr and the different peoples there living in the capitol, from all over the continent and across the sea. A desperate hope began to rise, she might blend in there. Her father was ambassador and travelled there often. Her brother had been with him when he'd disappeared.

Her resolve hardened, she was going to walk to Ackbarr and find out what had happened to Kaylan. Maybe her father would be there on court business or she might find someone who knew him. Rylan had said it took eight days, she could manage that. Her stomach rumbled and she tightened her belt as she stood. She didn't have much food, she'd have to go hungry for a bit.

She kept the mountains on her left as she walked, given a choice in roads she turned towards them. Rylan had mentioned Ackbarr was in the mountains. She tried asking the way from a pleasant looking older man looking after goats on the side of the road. His face became vacant on her questions, his mouth hanging open idiotically. She sidled back to the road, not knowing if it was her accent that was the problem or the information asked.

Mika stopped to look at the huddle of houses marking her first town since Fenin. A bustle of people moved through, it must be a market day. Her hesitation lasted for only a moment. She strode on, heart pounding, expecting a hand on her shoulder and a loud voice declaiming they'd found the murderer. Covered stalls were set out in the centre, people talking and carrying on their normal day to day living, while she ran in secret from the authorities. Her stomach grumbled as she passed the bakers, not daring to stop. She breathed out, hands shaking after she'd left the last straggle of houses.

She joined a number of people travelling on the main road for the planting further east. There were knots of strangers, travelling together for safety. Close enough to hear their careless talk and pick up snippets of conversation, she used them as camouflage. They in turn assumed she was one like themselves, content with her own company. The road was paved and wide, used by local traffic as well as horsemen. She was constantly on edge and nearly jumped out of her skin the first time she heard horses. Without enough time to hide she stopped, ready to face them and protest her innocence. They ignored her, sweeping by, treating her with the same disdain as they did the other travellers.

To add further insult, it started to rain. A fine drizzle that leaked through the cloak and made her sniff.

She knew she wasn't making much progress as the day wore on. A cart rattled by, she thought about hitching a lift and decided against it. At least with the rain and her hood up nobody gave her strange looks, just another weary traveller. The dye seeped from her hair, sinking into the cloak and shirt. She was dismayed to find her fingers came away a dark green when she ran her them through her hair. She kept her hood well pulled up after that.

The day grew darker as evening approached. No farmhouses to be seen, but there were plenty of trees to hide in. The other travellers stopped near hedges and woods, calling out to each other as they separated off into small groups. Mika didn't trust any of them enough to want to sleep close by. She choose a copse on the hill as her shelter for the night and plodded towards it, exhausted.

Mika no longer cared about hiding in the days that followed. She was lost. She'd not dared to buy food or ask directions in case she was recognised or remembered. She followed the mountains and the other travellers. All her good intentions about finding her brother and Ackbarr were lost in the haze of walking and worrying. The countryside was mostly grazing for sheep and cattle. Boys looking after livestock watched her walking with incurious eyes, one of many travellers on the road. The tiny villages were frequent and she would walk through each one in a panic, terrified of capture.

She ate the last of her food as the sun set, dragging the drab greyness into night. The mountains appeared no closer than they had been when she'd walked out of the city gates. Huddled in her heavy wet cloak under the thick canopy, she cried. Tears streamed done her face, as she desperately tried to work out what had happened that night. She had no memories, only the dreams of walking in the forest and hunting. It would be better to be an animal, with no worries, no cares, only the joy of the hunt. She remembered the iron taste in her mouth, the feel of her mouth closing around a small animal and felt sick, no longer able to tell her dreams from reality. Had it been her? Damp and exhausted she fell asleep, disturbed only by the sharp cry of a predator in the night.

Mika woke stiff in the morning, staggered to her feet and watched the road while the birds sang. She filled her stomach with water from a stream, set the mountains to her left and continued walking. The day was damp again. It was too early for berries and she didn't know what was edible around here. She had the coins she'd taken, but was too frightened to use them. At home it would have been easy. Home. Tears welled and she forced herself onwards.

There were no more villages that day, only the occasional farm. She was chased by a large white bird near the entrance to one. It hissed at her, spreading its wings and she stumbled away down the road.

Few horsemen pounded along the road now, either they'd misjudged her speed or had given up looking. She lost sight of the group she'd walked close to, no longer able to keep up. Others passed her without looking, absorbed in their own small miseries. Large barns and tiny cottages dotted the landscape. Small woodlands on the hills above the wide valleys and the bare fields waiting for a later planting.

By evening she was feeling light headed and sick. Another copse on a hill, she set her eyes on it and forced one foot forward then the other to keep moving in a weary plod.

Chapter 7

It was dark in the wood. She stood at the end of her strength, swaying as she tried to work out where to sleep. She thought she was dreaming when she heard the crackle and snap of a fire greeting her and the smell of food. Her mouth watered and without thinking she stumbled towards it. Mika stopped herself just before she walked into the clearing. People – mustn't go near. She gazed at the fire, the large tents and the horses picketed beyond. She could go faster on a horse. Could she steal one? Her brain refused to think.

A twig cracked behind her and she was slow in twisting away. A huge hand clamped over her mouth and another pinned her arms to her sides. They'd kill her, take her back to Fenin, she struggled through the exhaustion of the day. Her captor picked her up like a doll and carried her kicking and wriggling to the campfire.

An old man watched the fire while he sipped from his bowl. A number of servants were fussing around, making food and sorting out bags. She twisted, trying to wriggle some space between her and the guard. He solidly refused to let go, dumped her on her feet and held her up when they wouldn't hold her weight.

Mika heard the rumble in the man's chest as he addressed the old man, "Found something sneaking around."

She was held while the man calmly finished his soup. Her mouth watered at the smell. Wrapped in rugs against the damp, he was bare-headed, his pate holding only a few wisps of hair plastered down with rain. He was old, older than anyone she'd seen before. His hands were knotted and they shook as they held his bowl. She met his eyes dully, his were bird-like and gleaming with mischief. A servant held a napkin out, she noticed he dribbled.

"What are you doing at my campfire boy?" The old man's voice was strong despite the soft sound of few teeth. "Oh let him go Gavin, I think you're probably the only thing holding him up." The arms relaxed, but a huge hand kept hold of her upper arm. The old man glanced once at her captor and sighed. "Well boy?"

"I was hungry." That seemed a simple enough answer. He cocked his head, bright eyes examining her.

"Nice clothes, a little stained… interesting hair." She felt a tired indignation at his amusement. "There are a lot of men on the roads. We've come from Fenin. They appear to be hunting for something. Have you heard any rumours?" Mika shook her head, that was the truth. "Why are you on the road?"

She tensed further at the interrogation. Why? Her mind stumbled through every possibility, rejecting them all. She was too tired, she said nothing. He watched her, weighing her up and then abruptly said, "You seem like a bright boy. I am Belindros, have you heard of me?" The guard snorted softly behind her.

The name was familiar, memories coming back of her parents talking an age ago. "The Medici."

He beamed. "Well done. Your cheekbones and what might have been under the dye suggests that you are Cassai. Am I right?"

She hesitated, hating the thought of lying, "My mother was."

Belindros nodded, "Cassai have a reputation for integrity, have you inherited that with your mother's blood boy?" He laughed softly at her look. "I shan't make you answer." He seemed to come to a decision. "Let me see your hands."

Confused, she held them out and was dragged closer by his guard when he beckoned. He pulled them close to peer at them, turning them over. She hoped there weren't any blood stains left. "Hmm, slim, capable. How are you with blood?" Startled, she didn't know what to say. "Don't know? Well, how do you fancy being an apprentice to me? Think on it, it's not easy, lots of studying, gore and death, but it's worth it." The guardsman behind began to protest and was silenced with a look. "Well boy?"

Mika hesitated only for a minute, then desperate for the food she could smell, shrugged in what she hoped was a boyish manner. "Alright."

He snorted, she must have got the tone right. "My last apprentice died a few weeks ago in Dissan. He was asking questions in places he shouldn't have. I've no cure for stupidity." He looked disgusted. "His parents will be demanding to know what happened and I only took him on as a favour. I need someone bright, someone willing. Can you learn boy? Will your parents care?" Mika shook her head. He grunted and waved a hand, losing interest, "What did you use on your hair to make it so intriguing?"

"I don't know, it was a black powder, my last master used it to dye his hair."

"I think you'll find he used a mordant as well, it's gone green boy. And I can't keep calling you boy either, I like to know people's names."

She panicked. "Mi... Mikon."

He addressed the guardsman, "Give the boy some food, then take him to the stream. I've something that will strip the colour out in my saddlebags."

The guard hulked next to Mika and she tried not to stare as she saw him for the first time. No wonder she hadn't seen him in the dark, his skin was a deep blue black and his clothing looked a soft grey in the firelight, blending into the night.

"What's the problem? Flour on my nose?" His tone was teasing and she flushed as a servant gave her bread and soup.

"Where are you from?"

"Ackbarr." He grinned, challenging her lack of knowledge, then relented, "My parents were from Lannec. That's through the mountains, past the desert and over the sea to the northern continent to a geographically challenged Cassai boy." She nodded, eyes wide. Her country felt smaller than ever.

"Don't eat so fast, we've plenty of time." She tried to slow down, it was difficult to stop her hands shaking. The guard settled down more comfortably, watching as Belindros was helped up and escorted to a tent.

"Is that really Belindros?"

The guard chuckled, "Yes and he won't let anyone forget it. He's generally a good judge of people so don't let him be wrong, otherwise you'll have me to deal with as well." He offered a large hand. "The name's Gavin." The hand swallowed hers.

"What's a mordant?"

"Something that changes a dye to a different colour, we'll strip it off when you've finished inhaling your food."

A servant dropped a sachet onto her lap, "The dye remover young master."

The removing of the dye took a while, the powder was a bleach. Mika had hair nearly the colour of her fathers by the time it was taken off. Gavin assured her little of the green could be seen. She was shown to the previous apprentice's tent and given his cloak to wear while hers was dried. As Gavin left her, she asked where they were going.

"Ackbarr. Convenient for you?"

Mika nodded and said her good nights. She flopped into the blankets with relief. She was dry and warm, with food inside her. Going in the right direction with people who knew the way, it was a break from the bad luck. Her thoughts wandered as she remembered her father speaking of Belindros, passing on their conversations while talking to her mother.

The Medici, he was known everywhere as being high ranking in the King's court and equally for his intelligence and irascible temper. She'd heard others speaking of him, about his interest in their culture and the plants used for healing. Maybe, just maybe she would be alright. She stared at the bulky shadows in the tent, with the muddled thought that she hadn't expected him to be so old. Tiredness overwhelmed her and she fell asleep, not caring about tomorrow and the challenges of passing for a boy.

The next morning brought far more problems than her acting skills. She woke in the early morning, warm and dry, snuggled into the blankets. She relaxed for the first five seconds and stretched, anticipating curling up for a longer sleep when her insides curdled and turned to liquid. Clenching her backside she ran, pushing through the tent opening and nearly knocking over a sleepy servant in her haste. She reached the bushes, only just in time to unlace her trousers. Finishing, she walked gingerly back into camp, seeing Gavin look for her. A querulous voice was raised from the Medici's tent and Gavin answered quietly in his deep voice.

He raised an eyebrow, "Problems?" She explained, flushing and he grinned. "Probably bad water from a stream." He raised his voice to speak through the tent walls, "Lin, you got anything to stop Mikon sluicing his insides out?" The grumbling from inside the tent intensified. "Sit a while, you'll need to keep eating and drinking. Don't mind Lin, he's never good in the mornings."

"You a Medici too?"

He shook his head and laughed, "No, but I've picked up a few useful things here and there." A white powder was passed out which he mixed with the water heating on the fire. It proved to taste as disgusting as the resulting liquid smelt.

Eventually Belindros emerged in a vile temper, his joints aching. The servants and guards pandered to him, coaxing him to eat and sit out of the way as the camp was packed swiftly. Mika watched the gentle affection they showed for him and the acerbic comments he passed back.

Gavin grinned at her as he grabbed their saddlebags, "Ready to go?"

Mika nodded, then disappeared back into the bushes, despite not feeling as though anything else could happen.

Belindros smirked as she reappeared, "Better not slow me down boy, and keep washing your hands, nobody here loves you enough to want to catch it."

The last thing she wanted to do was to ride. Mika groaned as she pulled herself up and clung on, pleased for once it was a quiet horse. They set off at a gentle pace, punctuated by her scrambling down for the bushes. Gavin held her horse and waited. He helped her up, kept her drinking and told tales of worse dysentery until she snapped at him to shut up. He laughed and let her suffer in silence.

After a swift lunch, Belindros had a nap under a hastily erected shelter and was coaxed back onto his horse. She noticed that despite his age he sat well, his mare was well trained and responded to his movements with a light rein. He was stubborn and remained in the saddle until she could see it pained him and he had to be helped down for the day. The servants worked quietly around him, fussing gently.

As the camp was set up and Mika's insides began to behave themselves, Belindros ordered her to attend him. She sat waiting while he ate, took his bowls and napkins and answered questions about her knowledge. She soon discovered he expected her to think through ideas and give reasons for the answers, even if she wasn't sure. He asked her about the Cassai culture, the possibilities of war between Cassai and Ackbarr, although to her relief, he steered away from questions about her parents. She became fascinated by the depth of his knowledge and jumped when she heard Gavin's deep voice ask a question next to her. She turned to discover Gavin and a few other guards listening in.

She helped Belindros into his tent, turning him over to the servant's competent hands. The guards drew lots for the night watches, an easy camaraderie between them. The sky had grown dark and the fire was dying down, sending the tree shadows soaring. Mika had to remind herself that it was only a few nights ago that she'd been trapped within four walls, staring out at the life in the streets below.

Mika joined in with the packing the next day, helping Belindros without being asked and listened to the teasing, thinking how lucky she'd been. The day followed the same pattern as the previous and her stomach was feeling normal enough to panic when she saw the men on horseback coming from behind. Gavin loosened his sword and called the wagon to the side of the road.

The soldiers swirled to a stop around them and the sergeant came out to talk. Mika watched Belindros carefully move his gentle mare out to greet them. They made a study of contrasts, the aged man neatly dressed in plain robes, and the tall sergeant in his flashy uniform. After the first exchange of words it was clear who had the upper hand. The sergeant had made the mistake of demanding information and Mika had a ringside viewing of Belindros' temper when riled. He refused to let the sergeant get a word in, a gleam of dislike in his eye as he used every trick to confound him.

The sergeant's gaze fell on Mika and flustered, he used a gap in Belindros' barrage of words to grab her. "Where's this boy from? We're looking for a Cassai, he's got the right colouring for one." Mika froze, unable to work out which way to run. Gavin stood close by, outwardly relaxed, though his hand rested casually near the hilt of his sword. She winced, remembering her hair was pale as her father's, marking her out as different.

"That boy is my apprentice." Belindros' voice cut crisply through her thoughts. Mika's insides quailed as the sergeant looked sceptical. Why would Belindros shield her?

"How long have you had him?"

"Long enough to know that he is lazy and stupid, like any boy of that age. His parents foisted him on me, waste of fucking time if you ask me." Belindros' voice flicked out dismissively. Mika gaped, he thought she was stupid?

The sergeant turned to her, "Seen any other Cassai around boy?" She shook her head, still stung by the comments. He muttered under his breath.

"Why are you looking for a Cassai, sergeant?"

"A trader's been killed in Fenin. Large animal mauled all his family. A contingent of Cassai visited them a few months before. They've been seen sneaking around at other points too. Other places have reported a large animal savaging livestock."

"And you believe the Cassai are responsible?" Belindros' voice was soft and cutting.

"You know the rumours about Cassai." Under pressure from Belindros' withering stare the sergeant was reduced to spluttering, "I've heard them, about the King's Advisor."

"If I was given a copper penny for half the rumours I've heard about the Cassai, sergeant then I'd be rich and have a harem of big breasted women fighting over me every night of the week."

The sergeant's face was a picture. Mika could see him struggling to suppress the image conjured up by Belindros. He shrugged, starting to lose interest as he gave up. "I've had my orders to round up any Cassai for justice."

"Justice!" Belindros snorted, "Listen sergeant, the boy is part of my retinue. A fifteen year old boy doing what they do best – which is as little as possible. As Court Medici, I am answerable to the King only. Do you wish to speak to the King about my choice in apprentices?"

The sergeant backed down, bowing his head in defeat, "Medici." He turned back to his soldiers shouting, "Let's keep moving. Maybe we'll find something further on." A clatter of hooves and they were gone.

Mika breathed out in relief as Belindros looked after the soldiers in disgust.

"Let's move on while there's some daylight left. I want to be away from here and somewhere more secluded for a camp tonight." Gavin's tone allowed for no arguments.

Belindros nodded and turned to Mika, noting her face, "Cheer up boy, you're not as bad as I made out. Would you rather be riding with that sergeant to face his justice?"

That evening Gavin pointed out a deeper shadow on the mountainside ahead. "There's Ackbarr."

Mika gaped, it looked huge, she could just pick out the shape of a city in the mountain's curve. "We will get there tomorrow?"

Gavin shook his head, "It'll take a few more days. A courier changing horses could get there faster." He gestured to Belindros being helped down, muttering at his joints. "We have other concerns." Mika nodded and went to help.

Chapter 8

Mika watched the city come closer as they were slowly hauled across the wide river. Cries from fishermen and traders in the thin air greeted her. The wagon and horses came across in two journeys, the ferrymen yelling curses at the other boats shooting past.

Ackbarr, the place she'd heard about all her life and a place she'd never expected to see. Ranks of houses reared up in regiments in a crescent of the mountain and series of high walls marched between them. There were no slums here, the houses continued down to the neat docks by the river. Sewers carried away filth to the river and she heard rather than saw the livestock markets to the side of them.

Coming into Ackbarr from the bottom gate, they climbed constantly through the cobbled streets. Merchants and shop keepers raised their hands to greet the party and children ran after them, shouting for the delight of having Belindros eloquently comment back. The walls of the houses were dark granite, the shade was deep and streets narrowed by traders crying their wares. It had the look of a city built for war despite the people bustling around.

How could she have mistaken Fenin for Ackbarr? Gavin pointed out public buildings, libraries and temples. He teased her about being a country boy as she rode with her mouth open and wondered what her brother had thought, if he'd managed to ride in with his normal disdain for anything foreign.

People of all colours walked the streets, a few as blonde as herself, some closer to Gavin's polished ebony. Most had swarthy skin and flat features, dark eyes that flashed as they made deals, haggling on the steps and in the side alleys of Ackbarr. A large keep towered over the city. They rode close by and turned into a side street. There the group stopped and Belindros was helped down. She slid off, keeping hold of her horse, still trying to see everything.

Belindros made his way towards her. "Take this and go get yourself a proper haircut boy. Quick, before I mistake you for a girl and bugger you silly." Belindros sighed at the startled look on her face, mistaking it for shock. "You country boys, taking everything so seriously. Run along, go and enjoy yourself, explore for a bit. Make sure you find your way back here before sundown, otherwise someone will be buggering you and it won't be me."

Mika nodded, still slightly bewildered and accepted the small coins he gave her. She took note of the street in relation to the keep and wandered down the shady streets, tucking the coins into the purse inside her shirt. Old men sat in the dark openings to the houses, boasting to friends and drinking. Women bustled past, scolding and forcing them to give way with a dignified grumble. As she walked down the hill, the crowds grew. Children chased each other in complicated games of tag, shrieking and yelling. Stalls sprang up on each side, trinkets laid out on blankets. The street opened out onto a large square and she stopped close by a house wall to watch. So many people, shoving, talking, traders crying wares. The smell of bodies in the afternoon sun, rotting fruit, dogs sniffing. Overwhelmed, she stared, trying to work out where she could get her hair cut.

A tug at her sleeve, "Need a guide?" It was a child, no higher than her shoulder with a gaping grin. His bright eyes reminded her of Belindros.

"Yes, can you help? I need a haircut."

"Best barber in town, come on." He led her through into the cool side streets, Mika kept an eye on the stalls closest to orientate herself and followed. Her guide kept up a chatter the entire way, waving to people, traders, he appeared to be known by everyone. Many gave her an amused look, passing on good natured advice to her or curses to her guide. He stopped by an undistinguished doorway, stuck his head through and piped something. A roar greeted him and he skipped away as a large man lurched out.

"Needs a haircut." Butter now wouldn't melt as he pointed at Mika.

The man stumbled to a stop when he saw they had company. Mika looked on with dismay. He was foul. Bleary eyed, the fumes from drinking were obvious and his image wasn't helped by the long razor he held. At the sight of her, he drew himself upright with an unsteady dignity and disappeared back inside. Mika looked at the boy in confusion and jumped when a tall stool thumped on the ground.

"Sit. And you, sit somewhere else, out of my way." He pointed at the boy who grinned and curled himself against the wall, his pointed chin resting on his knees.

The barber took her chin and inspected her, "Don't need a shave, too young." He sagged a little, then went behind her and ran his fingers through her hair. He still held the razor, making her twitch. The haircut was swift and efficient, he used the razor to slice through, chopping her hair into the shaggy cut she'd seen on many others.

She paid him the price he grunted and asked, "Do you have anything to bleach hair?"

He gave her an odd look and shuffled inside, coming out with a paper package. "Don't use too much, you'll end up with no hair." She thanked him and nodded to her guide. They walked down the alleyway.

"Where now?" he asked.

Mika looked at his skinny frame and grubby face and said, "I think we'll visit a pie shop, I can see I have a friend that likes them." He grinned in reply.

They passed market traders who called out to her to buy their wares and shouted mock threats at her companion. His name was Jon, his mother had died several years back and his father spent most of his time drunk or indulging in shady dealing. He told this in a flat voice, scanning the marketplace as he spoke. He was younger than Petron, her little brother. She saw plenty of other children watching by the walls in the shade, their eyes dark with experience. Mika wondered how he'd missed out becoming like them.

They spent the remains of the afternoon walking round the market. Jon showed her the old city walls and they sat, legs dangling while they ate. Mika found that Jon's stomach was bottomless, she ended up giving him most of her pie when she saw him eyeing it.

The view from high up on the walls was incredible. The easiest way through the mountains was by boat Jon told her and Ackbarr blocked any trade unless the tariffs were paid. The immense cliffs behind the city were impassable and the river cut through the mountains and flowed below the city. Well-fortified docks on each shore and catapults for those traders who refused to pay. The river here was wide and lazy, there was no chance of a merchant shooting through. Ackbarr had grown rich on its taxes, enabling it to pay for subjugating the neighbouring provinces. Now it had turned its eyes on Cassai, Mika shuddered.

She could see the tiered ranks of houses had shallow roof pitches for standing on and firing at enemies, archways between buildings for defenders to run along. The streets were a confusing maze leading to the huge black fortress in the centre. The entire city had been built for defence, yet the people appeared open and friendly to foreigners like herself. She traced her journey on the road as far as she could see and wasn't sure she would ever get used to the wide open spaces beyond the city.

Jon nagged at her to talk about herself so she invented a brief tale about being apprenticed to Mekhi and finding him dead. Jon assured her that she'd done the right thing by running. Cassai were tolerated in Ackbarr city, but not so much elsewhere. She nearly laughed at his straight face and the worldly knowledge packaged in the skinny body of a street child.

The sun was beginning to go down when Jon finally brought her back to her street. He refused her coins, patting his stomach in appreciation. "I'll find you on your next day off." He scampered away leaving her smiling at his confidence. She didn't expect to have days off.

The door was large and sturdy, none of the usual rubbish left close by. A simple plate stated Medici, no name. She knocked and a woman older than her mother opened the door. With calm eyes, she accepted Mika's stumbling explanation of who she was and introduced herself as Marta, Belindros' housekeeper. Mika was shown around the house, the kitchen, outhouses and various examination rooms. Marta waved a hand at Belindros' study and private rooms as they passed. They climbed the stairs to the top of the house.

"This level will be yours." Two curtained alcoves were next to the door in the corridor, one held a privy, the other enough room for a bed. "This will be for your boy, when you have one."

The room for her was small, not much bigger than the cubby holes outside. A bed and a chest fought for space, there were old hangings on the walls and shutters at the windows. It had white plastered walls and dark beams above, with nails for hanging clothes.

"We don't have much space for apprentices. Lin has access to rooms in the palace, but he prefers to be here, it's quieter." Mika nodded, gazing at the tiny room. Marta hesitated, "Lin will expect you up early for lessons and you will probably have other tutors too. I haven't heard about his ideas for you yet."

"That's fine, I like learning."

Marta relaxed a little, "You don't mind the size? The last apprentice was constantly complaining."

Mika shrugged, "It's good for me."

The woman smiled and left. It got better when Mika realised the door had a lock. She opened the shutters and leaned out of the windows, peering down at the street below, listening to the cries of the traders. A good feeling welled up inside her. The house felt peaceful and someone was singing while they worked downstairs. She smiled, it couldn't get much better.

Chapter 9

Mika woke to the sound of a bell in the courtyard. She gazed at the rafters and grinned. Learning, lessons, all she had to do was pass as a boy, it couldn't be difficult could it? A knock at her door and she jumped out of bed to answer it, aware of only being in her shirt.

Marta stood there, "I don't normally come up, but you will need to be downstairs and ready to eat when the bell goes. Lin hates to be kept waiting and you'll end up with no breakfast otherwise." Mika nodded and dressed hurriedly, splashing her face with water.

She slid into the kitchen. The guards, including Gavin, were seated at a large table, laughing and joking. Gavin shifted over to give her space and introduced her to the rest. Mika sat in his shadow and listened. The banter was good humoured and mostly to do with teasing the youngest over his new girl. The kitchen staff waited on them, passing more food and drink as it was finished.

Marta caught Mika's eye when a small bell rang and nodded to her, "He'll be in the study, through the hall, second door on the right."

The doors in this part of the house were imposing, richly carved to impress clients. Mika brushed her knuckles across the wood, then built up her courage and knocked harder. She pushed open the door at the invitation and stared. Books, specimen jars and bones covered the shelves. A complicated water clock dripped quietly in the corner. The morning sunlight drifted in through the window, showing the view to the courtyard garden. Belindros sat at his desk, he wore his Medici robes this morning, making his ropey frame more imposing. He suited the room, a vast fount of knowledge resting in his eyes. A partially finished breakfast tray sat in front of him.

"Well boy?" She jumped and he smirked. "What do you think? Can you learn all this?" He waved a hand lazily at the room.

Unsure of the answer he wanted, she said "I can try."

He snorted. "Some of it is useful, a lot of it is crap." She stared, so many books, how could they be rubbish? "Experience boy, is what you need and using what is between your ears. Can you do that?"

"Yes."

"Good. There is a family which tutors some boys of about your own age nearby. You will be taking lessons with them during the afternoons. I expect to hear nothing but good reports from your teachers. Most mornings you will be with the apprentice Medici, learning elementary skills at the palace. Two evenings a week, Gavin will teach you rudimentary combat skills, more if you have an ability there. We will find your strengths and cater to them. Any questions?"

She hesitated, "I thought I was supposed to be your apprentice?"

Belindros laughed. "That ambitious already? Boy, you've not even started. I can't teach you anything until you've got the basics." He appraised her, making her squirm inside. "You will spend one morning a week in the examination rooms taking notes while I deal with my patients. Another morning you will follow around the wards at the palace hospice. Satisfied?" She nodded.

"Gavin will take you up to the palace and introduce you, it's up to you to get yourself there tomorrow. Again, I expect to hear nothing but praise from them. My last apprentice was foisted on me. Clung on like dog turd, smelt as bad too. Heard nothing but whinging from him. I don't need to keep you, understand?" He peered hard at her.

"Yes Medici." She understood. No parents to please, no need to keep her if she didn't match his expectations.

"Good, now bugger off and find Gavin."

She found Gavin waiting for her in the kitchen. Marta passed her an extra piece of bread and jam, saying something about boys and appetites. Mika noticed Gavin eyeing it as they walked and handed it over, she couldn't have eaten anything else, her stomach was too tight.

Sensing her worry, Gavin strolled up the hill towards the palace, pointing out the sights and telling tall tales until the palace gates came into sight. He introduced her to the sergeant on duty as Belindros' new apprentice. She tried to look intelligent and felt she'd failed when he merely grunted her through.

Gavin steered her on through the courtyard while she gaped. The keep was huge, it towered over the other buildings next to it. The doors were enormous, studded through with iron bolts. The scale was beyond anything she'd ever dreamed of. Her tiny country defied this? Mika had problems even thinking about going inside, let alone finding her father in there.

To her relief she didn't have to go inside, the hospice was to the side of the keep. A long low building with large windows and white washed walls. Inside it was fresh with an astringent smell assaulting her nostrils. She was met in the waiting room by an older boy wearing dark red robes. He took her name with a sober face and went to find the correct person.

Gavin cuffed her shoulder in a friendly way and left. A few other lads arrived while she waited. They peered at her from the corners of their eyes and she tried to ignore them as they scuffled around, poking and whispering. She noted their worn but decent boots and good quality clothing. These must be the servants of richer men, sent to pick up medicines. They quietened the minute the other boy reappeared.

"Through the curtain, turn right at the end of the corridor. Knock on the white door with Medici on it." Mika nodded as he turned to the next boy in the line.

She pushed past the curtains and entered the dim corridor, the building was quiet here, the outside world muffled and far away. Mika's insides were bouncing with nerves. She knocked at the door and entered.

It was a study, similar to Belindros'. A small man in the same green robes sat at the desk and smiled wearily at her. "You are Mikon." His voice was soft and deeper than she expected. "I am Abran. I've had a message from Belindros about you. You will be working and learning here in the mornings. I do not tolerate any misdemeanours from my students, any such behaviour is reported back to me and then to your sponsor, which in this case is Belindros. Do you understand?" She nodded, was it a pre-requisite for all Medici to look as though they could see through her?

"You do not have robes yet?" He sighed as she shook her head. "No doubt Belindros will sort them out for you shortly. Come with me."

He led her to another part of the hospital. Bottles of liquids were on the shelves, cupboards covered the walls and chests on the floor. A table was covered in long creamy strips of fabric, twisted and knotted from washing.

"These need rolling." He pulled a length out and swiftly rolled it, his fingers smoothing it into a neat bundle. "Sometimes a well rolled bandage can save someone's life. It can be needed swiftly, with no creases in the material to irritate the wound. Small details are important here, they can add into larger problems if we do not pay attention." She paid attention, his voice had fallen into a tone she recognised from the better of Kaylan's tutors. He was teaching her something.

"Do you have any questions?"

"Who were the boys in the waiting room attached to?"

Abran smiled, "Mostly minor nobles and traders. The more important nobles have Medici attend them. The poorer people will go to the hospices further down in the city. The journeymen Medici attend to them as part of their training. You will do the same at some point." The meaning was clear – if she got that far.

"But for the moment I roll bandages."

"Yes, the small important things. Show me, how do you roll a bandage?" He blocked her hands with his arm as she reached for them. "What have you forgotten?" Mika searched his face, looking for clues, had she failed already? He pointed to a tap coming out of the wall in the corner.

"Wash your hands before you touch anything."

"You didn't."

Amused by her pique, he picked up the bandage he'd rolled and dropped it on the floor. "Correct.

Bandages that need to be washed go into the basket in the corridor. Soap is by the tap." He watched as she put the discarded bandage into the basket and washed her hands.

He made several suggestions while she rolled the first few and then left her to deal with the huge pile. Her fingers grew tired as they pulled and tugged at the fabric. It was mind numbingly boring, her back ached with bending and she stretched, shifting her weight off her feet. She reminded herself that she'd escaped complete boredom in Fenin, she was going to be learning things and she had to prove herself to Belindros. The threat of being thrown out stuck with her through the morning.

Tears prickled her eyelids, everything had been happening so fast in the last few days. There'd been no time to think until now. They thought her father was responsible for the death of the trader. No mention of her. Her father was Cassai, it didn't matter that he was the ambassador. Had that been why they hadn't wanted her to go out in Fenin? Why Ardi had hated her? She decided that Ardi would have hated her whoever she was. She rolled with determination, tucking the bandages into the shallow trays as she'd been shown. The pile of bandages built up until she was pleasantly surprised to find she'd finished.

Mika stared around, unsure what to do next. Eventually she peered out into the empty corridor and sneaked back into the waiting room. The boy was still there, carefully writing something down.

"I've finished the bandages. What should I do next?"

His face twisted, thinking, "Can you write?"

"Yes."

"Rule up this sheet, then copy out this page." He handed her a sheet of paper and showed her the book he'd been writing in. "Anyone who comes in, we write their names in here, what they want and how much." Several lads arrived and left with medicines. She found it difficult with the strong city accent, different from the Fenin burr and the medicines were unfamiliar. A number of sounds changed how the letters were written down and she was dismayed at how many crossed out words she had on her sheet.

She was still writing when Abran came in. He blinked to find her in the waiting room. "You have finished the bandages?"

"I didn't want to disturb you sir."

"I am Medici, not sir and you will disturb me next time." The rebuke was gentle. He came to look over her shoulder and she winced at the mess on her paper.

"You are not used to writing our language. Ask when you are not sure, otherwise your hand is good. Carry on with Enos until lunchtime."

She sighed with relief when he'd left. Enos pointed out the spellings each time a boy came in after that and he encouraged her to ask the questions.

"What if they tell me the wrong things?"

Enos flicked a glance at her face, then her hair. "You are not a pauper here or a noble," He hesitated, "Or Cassai, you are Medici." A smile curled the side of his mouth, momentarily showing a mischief in his serious face. "The last page who deliberately gave the wrong information to a Medici apprentice spent a week on the privy. Word gets around." Encouraged, she started asking the questions, finding that all they did was glance at Enos first, then reply civilly. Her legs were aching by the time a discreet bell rang for lunch.

Lunch was simple, but filling with bread and a variety of cheeses and fruit. She discovered she was expected to have a strong stomach even while eating. One man read out symptoms from a book and apprentices raised their hands to answer the questions fired at them. The muted discussion under the eye of the journeyman Medici over the possible causes fascinated her, this was worth the hours rolling bandages. She kept her head down and listened hard.

Gavin appeared to take her to her next appointment. He laughed at her grumbling over her tired legs and her enthusiasm about the lunchtime discussion. When she started describing the various symptoms, he waved her away laughing, "No, I've learnt enough to keep me alive on the road. That sort of thing turns my stomach." He pulled faces and she realised with delight she had something to tease him back with.

They stopped in a street close to the keep. Again, Gavin introduced her and left. A servant regarded her, then inclined his head for her to follow. He opened a door further down the corridor, murmured something to the person inside and indicated she should go in.

She walked into a small room with nine students sat in rows all looking at her. With a shock she realised two of them were girls, they were all typical Ackbarr stock, dusky skin and darker hair. The deep brown eyes of the girls looked exotic to her. She felt very conscious of her pale hair and foreignness. She jumped as the tutor spoke and a chuckle ran through the class, making her flush.

"This is Mikon, he is Belindros' new apprentice. Treat him nicely, you may be needing his attentions at some point and no Tabat, not for any of the sexual diseases you intend catching in the near future."

Another soft laugh ran around the class and Mika sat at the spare desk indicated. She quickly found her history was lacking. Her brother had been taught Cassai history and he'd hated the subject, so she'd spent little time learning it. She was given a huge book to read and take notes from.

Again, she was involved in listening, so much to learn. This was better than she'd dared to dream of, she wouldn't have got this education in Cassai. Boys were lucky Mika decided, although remembering her brother's grumblings she didn't think they appreciated it. She was delighted to find that whilst the others gave the tutor as good as they got, they were still polite, making intelligent guesses when they weren't sure of the answers. She stumbled through a number of questions based on her reading and although there were a few grins, nothing more was said.

When Gavin came to pick her up late that afternoon, Mika was in a haze of exhaustion, her head spinning with information. He tucked her book under his arm and reminded her that she had combat practice with him later. At her protests, he simply pointed out that he was following Belindros' orders. She closed her mouth quickly, she couldn't let this beat her.

An hour after supper, she was regretting everything. She felt as though Gavin was slapping her around the courtyard for entertainment. He wasn't even hitting hard, just touching. She couldn't block him, couldn't stop him from tripping her up. She tried to remember the various throws and punches she'd picked up from Kaylan, but her body was tired and out of practice. The months of forced confinement showed and Gavin's style was nothing like she'd learnt from her brother.

It wasn't helped by the guards lounging around the walls, watching and passing comments. She doggedly put her head down and kept going, swallowing the humiliation. Eventually Gavin gave up, muttering that he'd had more of a fight with a five year old. She staggered upstairs to her bed and fell asleep with her clothes on.

Chapter 10

To Mika's delight she was given several changes of clothes, including the Medici robes. Belindros wore dark green, hers were apprentice red. The older, more tattered robes were for the palace hospice and she had a new set for special occasions. She'd noticed most of the apprentice's robes were worn in places but all had short sleeves, stopping at her elbow. Only the new set had the wide sleeves coming down to her wrists.

When she'd shyly asked Marta the reason why, Marta had laughed and said that the Medici had become fed up with the apprentices dipping their sleeves into everything and had cut them off. Mika loved the feeling of walking around in her new clothes, making her feel equal to the nobles in her tutor group. As Enos had said, people saw her clothing, not her features and pale hair. There was a muted respect in the local's eyes and they began to call greetings when she walked up with Gavin and the other guardsmen for their own training schedules. After a few days at the hospice, she was added to the roll call for Medici apprentice duties early in the morning.

Once a week, a journeyman Medici would teach the newer apprentices to make sure they were learning and adding to their knowledge. On the other mornings, Mika followed Enos around, holding bedpans, bandages and fetching simple things. Whilst he wasn't the brightest of students, being the fourth son of a very minor noble, Enos was desperate to prove himself.

He rolled his eyes as yet another member of his family left them, having picked his brains for a minor ailment. His family made the other apprentices laugh, constantly calling on him rather than the journeymen Medici down in the city. Even Abran appeared to tolerate them with amusement, sending them to Enos in his breaks. When Mika asked about them coming to see him, he explained his other option had been joining the priesthood.

Enos looked disgusted, "At least I'll get the chance to kiss girls as a Medici." His father had persuaded a low ranking Medici to sponsor him after Enos had protested against becoming a priest. She laughed with him and he told her that what he really wanted to do was travel.

"You can be on the move constantly, new people, places every day." His eyes shone at the idea of finally getting away from his family.

If Enos' teaching was slow and exactingly correct, her mornings with Belindros were entirely different. She watched with fascination his technique with patients, his acerbic tongue tamed as he reassured them, exuding a calm confidence. He was constantly talking and explaining while she sat and made notes in the corner. She was expected to notice everything and would be quizzed afterwards. He wanted to know about the patients, what they were wearing, how he had responded to their symptoms and why. She realised at one point how lucky she was, his enthusiasm overflowed when teaching and no question was ever too daft not to answer.

On her first day off Mika found a tailor willing to sell her several corsets for her 'sister'. These she modified to strap her breasts flat and felt thankful they weren't big. She wondered when her bleeding would start again and bought bandages in anticipation. These she figured she could wash without too much bother. She was in a Medici's household after all, bloody bandages were a fact of life. She learnt to strip wash in her room, avoiding the bathhouse. Gavin at points offered to take her out and "make a man of her". He chuckled at her refusal, assuming shyness.

Mika's days blurred into each other, trotting from palace to tutor room, the guards at the keep nodding her through without comment. She became used to the size of the vast complex, finding her way around and ignored the keep towering over her.

She began to distinguish between the other boys she learnt with in the afternoons. Rufus was the natural leader of the group, confident and secure in his position. Tabat was the clown, she'd noticed most of the tutor's comments were aimed in his direction. Lissina's father owned the house they learnt in and Jenna her friend. They were all wary of Mika to begin with, not ignoring her, but cool. They were too well bred to exclude her openly, however she was not included in the outings they spoke about amongst themselves.

The teachers were broad-minded when it came to the girls education, in fact, they shared all the lessons. She could see why her father had tolerated her learning with Kaylan, he would have seen the noblemen's daughters here. They would be expected to be able to defend and deal with their husband's estates while they were away and needed to be taught so, much to the surprise to the boys who obviously hadn't thought about the capabilities of their own mothers. Crossbows were Jenna's speciality, everyone ducked or got out of the way when she picked one up, the look in her eye said it all. Even Jenna smiled when the tutors made comments about her future husband treating her with care. Mika had a pang of regret, she would have enjoyed laughing and learning with them as a girl.

As one of the teachers had said, "Right gentlemen, I've heard you muttering. So, why do we have the young ladies in the strategy sessions? Why not just let them get on with needlework like the rest of the girls in the city?" He stared around the group and they hushed in anticipated delight. "Why? Because young Rufus, when you are married to one of them and are between their legs, you want them to be giving you good advice. Presuming first you are listening and second, that you will have got between their legs in the first place." Mika joined in the laughter, watching how the boys reacted, their body language, how they sat and imitated them.

Mika had lessons in fencing as well as medicine and science, maths and languages. She had the edge in language, speaking and writing two helped. To her disappointment, Cassai was not one they were expected to learn. The two girls kept the other boys on their toes, proving they could keep up both intellectually and also physically with the fencing lessons.

Staring down the point of a rapier into the laughing face of another girl wasn't funny and she didn't have the weight to push through like the boys did. Fencing was a skill she'd not learnt with her brother and it took a concentration that left her sweating. She focused on her lessons with Gavin, finding what worked best for her. Her fitness improved with the lessons from Gavin and he regularly paired her off with another guard to see her technique. With her days full she had no time to think about Fenin. Her dreams were fuzzy with deep sleep, wrapped up in the learning of the previous day.

Weeks turned into months of lessons before she knew it. Ackbarr had a gentle temperate climate, sheltered by the mountains and the seasons turned slowly. The winds blowing off the plains fed warm air into the city. Late summer was approaching, the hot sunlight reflecting off the black walls and dipping low off the rooftops in the evenings with spectacular colours.

Belindros called her into his office one morning. "I've had the reports on you. I'm pleased." Never one to beat about the bush, he carried on, "You may have noticed the other apprentices have boys to train. I think you can manage one now."

Mika gulped. She'd seen the boys, about twelve years old running around. They looked a handful. Some were boys wanting to become apprentices, like Enos, with their families hoping to catch the eye of a Medici to sponsor them. Most were the sons of noblemen, their fathers looking for them to learn a few skills for minor wounds on the battlefields. She would be expected to keep them learning and out of trouble.

He smirked at her discomfort, "Come with me to the palace, I'll introduce you and you can decide in the next week or so. It doesn't have to be one of them, but it's usual. Do your best to keep their noses clean. Pain in the arses, the lot of them."

They walked slowly to the palace, Belindros talking further on his expectations of the boy she would teach. He interrupted himself to wave at a few scantily clad ladies leaning out of a window, they waved back blowing kisses. "Look at those women, just look at them." Belindros sighed as he noticed the reluctance on her face, mistaking it for shyness. He shook his head, "Damn it boy, you've got the youth, I've got the willing. I'd swap everything for a day in your flesh." Mika stifled a giggle at the thought of Belindros using her body and sobered, thinking about what his reaction would be to her true sex.

Belindros showed her the boys – none of them appealed. They were all superior, knowing their places and bored of the lessons, no spark. She anticipated having problems with all of them.

"Watch them for a while, see who you like." Belindros left with a smirk for her discomfort.

Mika tried, they were all so sure of themselves she thought in despair. They were polite when she asked them to do things and silently smug at her struggles. Hesitantly Mika picked a boy that looked bright and tidy for his age. Orai was twelve, confident in his abilities and talkative. After only a few days, he was running rings around her and she'd got fed up with supervising him.

High spirits were one thing, but he constantly wound her up, she couldn't get him to do anything, trust him with anything. Everything broke in his hands. He refused to sleep in the cubby hole, had to go back to his parents every night and came in late every morning. His eyes grew wide at any accusations she made, until her own eyes stung at night with frustration. Mika thought of the other Medici apprentices and how careful their boys were. She'd been saddled with a brat. She was starting to agree with Belindros about boys and their habits.

Jon had whinged about her deliberately missing him on her first afternoon off. He caught her on the way to the palace a few days later, telling her that he knew all apprentices had time off. He winkled out when the next one would be and waited at the gates to the courtyard. She thought at first, he was just there for the pies she bought. When he kept finding her, she realised he also liked talking to her. In return he took her all over the city, insisting first she remove her robes and showed her the places she'd never have dared go near on her own. Even there he was known, a grudging smile or grunt in his direction and the kick or cuff often restrained at his piping comments.

She grumbled about Orai to Jon.

"Show him who's boss then."

"I try, he doesn't listen."

"If I don't listen then I get a hiding. It's simple." Jon's face crinkled, not understanding.

"I can't hit him, he's the same age as my little brother, I wouldn't hit Petron."

Jon shook his head, "You're going to have to do something." He changed the subject, "Have you seen the new pie trader?" Mika laughed and went with Jon to find him.

Primal forest with huge tree trunks, dim light and the muscular grace of a large predator sliding through the undergrowth. Mika twitched, caught up in her dream. Moss and still pools, gnats swarming above. The crashing of beasts in the distance and the humming of bees. Birds in the trees sounding their alarm calls. Threading her way through, her viewpoint low, blinking in the green light. No concern of getting lost, there were too many signposts in the featureless forest. She woke sweating, her muscles tense and trembling.

Mika wondered about that night in Fenin, remembering how upset and frustrated she'd been. Still confused over what had actually happened, she analysed every aspect she remembered. All she could recall was the intensity of the dream she'd had and the feeling of being in something else's flesh. She checked her lock, making sure it was secure and feeling ridiculous, tried making herself angry. It didn't work. She lay staring into the dark and gave up, disgusted with herself for encouraging a fantasy.

As she grew less tired, she began to dream more, they happened intermittently, building up and then dispersing. Kept awake one night worrying, she remembered her mother tucking sachets of vineflower under her pillow for sweet dreams. She found the sachet she'd brought from Fenin and a faint scent came out when she scrunched it. Mika breathed in deep and found herself relaxing at the smell of home and safety. Her sleep was dreamless that night.

As the months went by, she settled into a rhythm, the lessons, learning at the hospice and free time with Jon. Her stamina improved until she could keep up with Gavin and the guardsmen began to make approving noises. She discovered she was fast, able to whip through her opponent's defences. She started to incorporate Cassai techniques that Gavin hadn't met before and Gavin found her a fencing instructor to practice with, correctly guessing she would be better with the lighter weapon. As she pointed out smugly, she was going to be a surgeon, not a butcher.

Chapter 11

To her surprise Rufus invited her to join the other students after lessons one day. They larked about in the parks, bought pasties and teased the girls. She delighted in finally messing around with those of her own age, a welcome distraction from the constant lessons. Mika kept having to remember she was a boy, not simply in a similar group with her brother. Joining them became a regular fixture and Jon gave her the time with reluctance. She'd see him on occasions hanging around on the street corners and would wave discretely and he'd grin back, pleased to have been noticed.

Rufus came into lessons one afternoon, full of a secret. He kept them waiting, hinting he knew something everyone else didn't. The tutor left with a smile at the suppressed excitement.

"They've caught that cat, didn't you hear? The one that was killing everything in the countryside between here and Fenin." Rufus couldn't keep it in any longer.

The others crowded around, excited. Jenna joined in, "The King's Advisor had to help in the end. I heard father talking about it this morning."

Mika wanted to know more, "What cat?"

"They couldn't catch it..."

"Too clever by half..."

"Outwitted all the hunters…"

"It's huge I heard..." The comments came thick and fast, admiring the animal.

"I thought you didn't have big cats here?"

They shrugged, not caring. Rufus, still bursting told them, "They're bringing it in today, putting it in with the others. The King's Advisor's going to be there."

The talk swirled around her and ignoring her questions, they plucked at Mika to come in their excitement. It was agreed they would go to the menagerie to watch. She'd not been there before, it cost to get in and was only accessible to the nobility. Rufus blagged them in, using his father's name. There were many cages, some larger and fuller than others. Mika wanted to stop and look at the exotic animals, she was sucked along with the others. They stopped in front of the largest cage, a crowd was already there, murmuring excitedly.

Mika felt sick when she recognised the big cats from her country. She'd never seen one in the flesh, only read and heard about them. They were shy of people in their normal environment. The sleek, grey fur shaded to tan, green eyes, blues eyes, flicked at the crowds as they paced and stared. This cage was complete and enclosed over the top to stop any chance of jumping over. There were a few half-hearted attempts at foliage and some rocks for them to lie on. Her heart ached, they looked bored, she could feel it, pulling at her.

A louder muttering ran through the crowd and something red and jagged ran through her brain, pulsing. Mika gasped, trying to stay on her feet, the crowd pressing around her. The area felt too hot, too full of people, she pulled at her collar trying to get some cooler air in. Emotions washed over her that weren't hers, there was an anger and an indignation of being enclosed. Her skin shivered in sympathy, she wanted to get out but the crowd hemmed her in, elbowing her back.

Soldiers arrived, shouting warnings and pulling a large cart that rocked. Something thumped against the inside, its occupant clearly unhappy. Keepers ran next to it, clearing the way and warning people to keep back. Mika staggered and the red fury turned into a pounding headache. The noise of the crowd seemed to switch off as they pushed the wooden box up to the cage. She watched in silence, seeing the other cats turn to stare, fur bristling. The feelings intensified as their lips drew back and eyes slitted in anticipation of an intruder.

The keepers slid the door of the box up, the same with the cage door. An excited murmur from the crowd which hushed as they waited. Nothing happened. The keepers poked a stick in through the back end and a cat sprung out. Mika caught her breath - it was beautiful. The sun shone on its fur, the muscles rippled, its ears were back and its face set into a mask of hatred. It was lithe and muscular, a jungle cat, there to hide and stalk through the forests... she felt dizzy with the emotions pushing through. Its movements screamed at her, it shouldn't be here, not for people to stare at.

A cat sprang at the intruder and taken by surprise it jumped a clear ten feet away with ease. Another stalked it from the other side. There were yells of encouragement from the audience. Through her headache she could do nothing but watch the crowd in its bloodlust, even her friends were shouting, caught up in the excitement. Swipes of red bloomed on grey sides...

A yell and the crowd parted reluctantly. Her attention was dragged away from the cage. A tall hooded man was arguing at the keepers. A ripple of conversation as people noticed. His back was to her as he gestured to be let in. She flinched as a blow from an unsheathed paw landed and felt rather than heard the squeal. The keepers were refusing, the soldiers shrugged, if he wanted to go in… A fist flashed and the crowd were delighted as a keeper went down. The man shouldered the box aside, ducked through the cage door and pulled it shut behind him. The cats continued to stalk their new companion, too busy to notice another intruder.

The man strode up and grabbed a cat by the scruff of its neck as it prepared to spring, knocking it to one side. It turned to snarl, then cowered. A numbness spread across her mind and she began to focus more. The other cats noticed the man and slowly backed away. He was left facing the newcomer.

Mika was aware of Rufus talking excitedly in the background about the King's Advisor. She ignored him, staring as the man walked up to the new cat. It snarled and crouched, tamping its hind legs down. His stance showed no fear as the cat twisted itself in readiness to spring. All sinuous curves and lashing tail, its claws unsheathed. A jagged line of pain ratcheted across her brain and it was met by a mental buffet so hard she staggered. Lissina turned to make an excited comment. Her eyes were shining, not noticing Mika's distress. Mika barely noticed the cat staggering through the ache in her skull. She concentrated on standing straight, trying not to vomit.

Roles reversed, the cat backed off, wanting to gain distance from the man that stalked it. Both ignored the shouting crowd and the other occupants of the cage. The intensity of its gaze, muscles rolling smoothly under the fur and it leapt. Another blow in her mind and Mika's cry of pain was lost in the shout of the audience. The man moved, shifting as the cat twisted in the air trying to reach him and it failed. It stumbled inelegantly, the blows raining down against Mika's mind, jarring her and the man moved again. Grabbing the cat by the scruff of its neck, he pulled its jaw up to stare into its eyes. The crowd fell silent. Nothing moved in the cage. Mika felt sick, barely standing, ignored, waves of nausea passing through her. Limply she let them, allowed it to wash through, over and past her.

She gazed through exhausted eyes as the cat slowly rolled to the ground giving way, its tail thumping and ears bent back. The sickness passed. A long pause, then the man stood and clicked his fingers. Mika could feel the tightening of the mental noose around the cat. It slunk to its feet and the crowd gasped as it pressed close to the side of his leg. He briefly ran his fingers through the soft thick fur over its neck then walked to the door of the cage, the cat padding beside him.

Mika stared as the man turned and his hood slid down, she'd expected the flat faced features of Ackbarr. He was Cassai, tall and long limbed. After a short argument the door was opened and the crowd shrank back. He eyed the mass of people, arrogant in victory until his eyes caught her hair. A flicker of shock between them as his eyes pinned hers, then he ignored her to walk away, the cat following at his heels.

Mika sagged, Lissina was looking at her strangely and she did her best to pull herself upright. She'd been sweating all through the encounter. "Who was that?"

Tabat sniggered, "That was Jace, the King's Advisor for War." He puffed himself up and walked in imitation as the crowd dispersed. The others laughed.

"He's Cassai. I thought they weren't allowed positions of power in Ackbarr."

"He's not Cassai or at least not full blooded, he can't be, just look at his hair. He's not even as blond as you and you're only half. My father says he's too damn good at fighting to be left hanging around. Someone else would snap him up otherwise." Rufus was full of his father's knowledge as they began to walk back.

He was Cassai and what's more she knew, unlike those boys, that Jace must be closely related to the Cassai royalty. His features were similar to her mother's, the sandy hair exactly the same shade and those eyes, the power in them, she shivered.

The boys were sniggering about Jace, "There are rumours about what he does with those cats, haven't you heard?" Delighted to be informing a new pair of ears, they chose the crudest possible terms, leaving nothing to her imagination.

It finished with Tabat saying, "Licks his balls clean after fucking, twists around, just like a cat." She was forced to laugh with them, despite her tight head. The boys pushed and shoved one another, laughing and making rude cat sounds. Mika noticed Lissina looking thoughtful.

Lissina shrugged when she asked. "I think he's interesting, just look at what he did with that cat. You two look quite similar, did you know that?"

Mika's answer that most Cassai looked like her was lost under the boys hooting. They teased Mika to be careful of Lissina all their way home, suggesting ways to "tame the pussy", in all its possible connotations.

She slept badly that night. Her dreams were full of the memories of the cat and the man. His mocking

113

eyes coming closer, the jolts of power twisting her body, forcing her to do his bidding. She whimpered as she felt her body want to stretch and without knowing why, fought it. Halfway through the night she got up and found her mother's sachet of vineflowers. Pressing it against her nose, she thought of her mother and calmed, sleeping like the dead for the rest of the night.

Cranky and tired, she stumbled down in the morning. Orai grinning, sent her up to Belindros' room, having assured her that she was wanted. Without thinking she went and to her surprise the door opened. Belindros stood in the middle of his room, his arms wrapped around a plump middle aged woman. Mika blinked and couldn't help staring.

"Piss off Mikon. Haven't you ever seen a pair of tits before?"

The older woman turned her head away. Sure that she was laughing at her face, Mika flushed and shut the door quietly. She'd had enough of her trainee, she scowled and decided she was going to get rid of him.

Mika stalked downstairs, grabbing a willow switch from a basket near the fire. Orai looked up, smirking as she came in, positive she wouldn't do anything. She composed her face and walked past. He sniggered and then yelped as she whipped the switch across his back.

"You know I'm allowed to beat you black and blue, don't you?" Orai went pale, she'd never lost her temper before. "Get out," she said quietly.

He scrambled off the bench, the others studiously ignoring them. She flicked the switch over his backside and he ran for the courtyard. White faced, Orai tried to wriggle away and she had to get him in an armlock to keep him in one place. All her frustration over his behaviour and the sleepless night came out at once as she raised her switch. He whimpered and she caught sight of his face. Petron's image came into her mind and she shut her eyes, trying to block out how she'd feel about someone doing the same to him.

Mika gritted her teeth and brought the switch down - he had to learn to behave. Orai squealed at the air whistling as it narrowly missed him. She dragged him upright and stared hard into his eyes, "Between you and me, I've beaten you silly. You know I can and you don't want it, do you?" Orai shook his head violently, eyes wide.

"Just remember, the next apprentice may not have as much patience as me. I'm taking you back to Abran." He scrambled away and got his things when ordered.

Back in the kitchen, she was greeted with good cheer and teasing over finally having disciplined her charge. She'd not dared ask about Belindros and his woman, her cheeks flushed every time she thought about it.

Orai was still snivelling when she marched him wet legged back to the palace. In the end, that was enough punishment. The other boys sniggered when they arrived, Mika holding Orai firmly to stop him cringing away. Abran merely raised an eyebrow before accepting Orai back. He politely enquired if she would like another trainee. She shook her head, she had other ideas.

Chapter 12

Jon rubbed his nose and waved as Mika greeted him. He'd been throwing pebbles at the wall and kicking his heels while he waited for her. They walked towards the market square while Mika worked out the best way to approach him with her proposal. "Do you like it where you are?"

He looked around, "S'okay."

"No, not here. I mean living in the market and with your father. Do you like it?"

His face turned sulky, "Doesn't matter does it?"

"If you had a chance to get out, would you take it?" His small face crinkled and she rushed on, "I've been asked to find a boy to train up as an apprentice. I don't like any of them. I've had this brat for the last month, he was terrible. I had to stop myself from beating him silly yesterday. I think you're far more capable. Would you do it?" He didn't look impressed. "Yes, it would mean working hard, but it would also mean food and somewhere safe to sleep."

"I don't do charity." He was stiff, she could see he thought she'd insulted him.

"It's not charity. I think you're bright. You'd have to learn things that the other boys already know, like reading and writing, but if you stick at it, you could become a Medici."

"You need a sponsor to get that far."

"I get paid a small amount. I'll work something out if you're interested."

At least he was listening now. "Why me?"

"I told you, you're bright. I don't like those other boys, they don't want to learn, they don't need it. You'll also get fed, at least three times a day." Marta had a thing about boys being hungry, Jon would be given more food than he could cope with.

His face twitched, she had him there, he was permanently hungry. Catching her glance he laughed, "You're desperate."

"Tell me you're twelve."

"I'm twelve." His eyes were guileless, "Why?"

He didn't look twelve, his skinny body couldn't be more than ten, but maybe she could say he was starved and would catch up in size.

"You need to be twelve, everything else we can deal with. Well, will you?"

He shrugged, feigning disinterest, "I'll try it. Did you mention food?" She chuckled and turned to walk them back home.

Gavin was working out, using his heavy wooden training sword as they came into the courtyard. He stopped and leant on it, sweating in the still air.

"Hey Mikon, where'd you get the monkey? You know pets aren't allowed."

Mika snorted. Before she could reply, Jon piped up, "Watch it big stuff, I got a knife."

Gavin laughed and choked out, "I'm scared, don't threaten me, can't you see my knees are knocking?" He turned serious, "Mikon, Marta isn't going to be pleased with you bringing him into her kitchen." Mika shrugged and dragged Jon off to the bathhouse.

Jon stared at the pool, "I've been here before."

"Yeah right. Now, strip and wash yourself. That's soap, use it and wash all over. I'm going to be checking."

"I don't remember anything about baths being part of this." Jon turned stubborn.

Mika took a breath to reply that he had to be clean, when a shadow came in the doorway and they both turned to see Marta standing, her arms folded.

"Jon, I remember you from when your mother came here to wash clothes for me." His mouth hung open, Mika hadn't seen him lost for words before. Marta turned to her, "Gavin told me that I might want to see what you'd brought in."

"I don't like any of the boys Belindros wants me to take on." Marta nodded as she stumbled for words. "They all seem so sure of themselves, too proud and looking down on me, I can't teach them."

"The idea is that you learn how to get them to do as you want, before you start on the patients. Not everything is easy Mikon. You think a street child would be easier?"

"Jon's bright, he can learn."

"It won't be easy. Jon, you will wash yourself, I will be checking." Jon nodded, unusually subdued. Marta drew Mika out of the room. "I knew his mother, she was a good woman. I lost contact with Jon after she died. Do you understand what you are doing?"

"Doesn't he deserve a chance?"

"He's a street child, do you know what habits he has?" She saw Mika bristle. "Yes, you might enjoy your days off with him and I can see why, he was an engaging child three years ago, but now." She shook her head. "You realise he's only ten. He's younger than the others, less educated and smaller. Is this fair on him?"

"I like him."

Marta sighed, "Well, I shan't say anything about his age, but it's up to you to keep him in line."

Jon appeared with a towel wrapped around his skinny body. His skin showed several shades lighter and the tide marks showed he'd had an honest attempt at washing. Marta took hold of an ear and inspected him as he wriggled. "I will get you a new tunic, then Mikon will de-louse you and you can eat before you see Belindros." Jon muffled his squeak of protest at the mention of food.

Marta showed Mika the disgusting process of the nit comb. They ended up cutting off most of Jon's hair, while he whinged that they were pulling it out. When they'd finished, what was left curled slightly, static from the combing.

Gavin wandered in, "Whoa, the monkey's had a bath!" Jon spluttered swear words in his direction.

Marta stopped him with a look. "None of that in here please."

Jon's eyes fixed on the pie she held and assumed his best angelic look, Mika smothered a laugh, it didn't work with his sticky out ears and pinched face. His eyes followed the pie as it was deposited into Gavin's large hand. Gavin grinned at him, took a bite and sauntered out.

"You will behave here," Marta continued. She picked up another pie, Jon's nose twitched and he nodded energetically. She gave it to him and it was finished in short order. Licking his fingers, he looked around for more.

Knowing Jon's appetite for anything edible, Mika stood him up despite his protests that he was still hungry. "We'll see Belindros next."

Belindros was in his study, he answered the knock with a mumble. They entered to find him next to the window, a book held close to his face. "What does this say boy?"

Mika picked up the book and read out the paragraph he pointed to. He grunted, "Thought so, nothing wrong with my memory. Fucking Varian, thinks he knows everything. What is that next to the door?"

Mika followed his gaze to Jon. Her insides curdled at his tone, "That's Jon."

"Do you need a pet? I'll get you a ferret if you like, they eat less." He sniffed, "And smell less too. Has it been boiled?"

"You said I could choose a boy to teach and it didn't have to be one of the boys from the palace." He was silent, staring down his nose at Jon and she ploughed on, "I don't like any of them. Jon's far brighter and he wants to learn."

"You can teach ferrets too. They catch vermin. Probably about his size. How old is it?"

"Twelve." This was going worse than she thought.

Belindros snorted, "If that thing's twelve then I'm eighteen tomorrow."

"Congratulations sir." Mika winced and screwed up her face trying to shut Jon up. "Only a few years to go and you can have your majority."

Belindros eyed him, "Lippy little shitter isn't it? I've a cure for that." He walked back to the table and picked up a needle and a reel of thread. Jon raised his chin and stared back.

They stared each other out until eventually Belindros harrumphed and waved a hand, "Make sure I don't hear anything bad about your ferret, otherwise it's got an appointment with my dissecting table." Mika looked blank. "I've a mind to find out how those bones animate without any muscle on them."

Mika hastily thanked Belindros and bundled Jon out into the corridor before he could answer back.

She escorted Jon upstairs and showed him the cubby hole, "This is yours, there's space here for clothes, you can put books here. I know it's small..." She trailed off as Jon stood with his mouth open.

"Mine?"

"Yes, we'll need to change the sheets. They stink of Orai, despite him never having slept in them. Look, you take that end of the mattress."

Jon slowly took the end and pulled gently, "All mine?"

"Yes."

"I've never had a place of my own to sleep." His face was comical, she almost laughed and then realised he was serious.

"You'll have to work for it like I do. Learn to read and write and everything." He nodded slowly as she showed him how to take the cover off the pillow.

Marta saw her as she brought down the dirty sheets. "Well?"

Mika sighed, "Well, he didn't say no."

"Where's Jon?"

"In his room. I think he's worried someone will take it away from him if he leaves it."

Marta laughed gently with her, "I'll get a change of clothes for him, the less the other children can make fun of him the better." Another point Mika hadn't thought of.

"When can I start teaching him? I don't have much spare time."

"I'll talk with Lin. He may make allowances."

Jon quickly became part of the household, helping Marta in the kitchen during the day and having lessons with Mika in the evenings. He was bright as Mika had suspected and he became a favourite with the guards. He tagged along behind Gavin and most afternoons the small boy could be found sitting close to the large warrior. Mika frequently had Gavin's outrageous stories re-told to her by Jon later in the evenings, with his own extravagant comments added to the mix.

"What's that smell?" Mika stuck her head into Jon's cubby hole one morning. She'd noticed a smell in there a few times recently.

Jon sat on his bed looking worried, "Nothing."

"Jon it stinks. You'll have Marta in here." She reached down to pull back the mattress, "Bloody hell Jon..." There was food mashed underneath, slowly rotting. Jon looked helpless.

"Did you take this? What's up, aren't you fed enough?" Jon had been eating enough for two at mealtimes. He started stammering, trying to explain, tears coming into eyes. All of a sudden, he wasn't the cocky little boy she was used to, he was scared. She let the mattress down with a damp thump and sat next to him. "What's up?"

"I don't know." He huddled next to the wall, refusing to look.

"Are you hungry?"

"No." His head was hanging. "Are you going to throw me out?"

"No."

"I messed my bed."

She thought hard, he'd been so proud of his room. "Look, do you need to keep food here, just in case?" He twisted away from her, not wanting to meet her eyes. "I could get something from Marta, something bottled so you know it's there and it can't rot. As something to fall back on. You can tuck it away so no one can see it. Would that help?"

Jon, tense and miserable, slowly nodded. Mika desperately wanted to give him a cuddle like she would her little brother. She had to remind herself that she was a teenage boy and settled for giving him a hair ruffle instead.

"OK, I'll get a bowl from the kitchen. I'll scrape the worst of this off and we'll take the mattress down to wash and dry it in the courtyard. We're lucky it's sunny today."

He sniffed and wiped his face on his sleeve as Mika hurried out of the room and grabbed a bowl from the kitchen. Marta raised an eyebrow from where she was cleaning shelves and supervising the servants.

"Jon needs some bottled preserves, do you have any spare?" Marta nodded and passed a couple of jars down from the top shelf. Jon had peeled the bedclothes off by the time Mika had got back. He was still sniffing.

"Right, these are yours. No diving into them unless it's an emergency."

He managed a shaky grin. Together they man-handled the mattress downstairs. Mika gently began teasing Jon about having eyes bigger than his stomach while they sluiced it down. He sniffed his way through his retorts and looked far happier by the time they'd finished.

Chapter 13

Mika crept down to the infirmary early, looking for bandages. With regular meals and exercise, her monthly cycle had settled down quickly. She'd run out of clean bandages by accident yesterday having washed them too late. She normally dried them in the warmth of the chimney breast coming up from the kitchen. Keeping them out the way of Jon was difficult, he was too curious and never having had a place of his own, he didn't understand her need for privacy. He'd eventually agreed to stay out of her room, but it didn't stop him from trying to peer in whenever she opened her door.

She rummaged through a pile and found one the right length and thickness, tucked it into her pocket and jumped as she saw Marta in the doorway.

"I thought I heard someone in here. Why do you need the bandages? Is Jon alright?" Mika hesitated, she couldn't lie to Marta, she liked her too much. Marta appraised her, then came inside and pulled the door shut. She sat on one of the high stools, "Talk to me."

Tears came into Mika's eyes, she couldn't lie about this. She blurted out, "I'm not a boy, I'm a girl. I need them for... you know..." She hung her head, not looking, waiting for Marta to call Belindros and be thrown out. Maybe someone else could take Jon on, maybe Marta would as a kitchen boy if nothing else.

Mika jerked her head up as Marta laughed softly, "I was wondering why you were so secretive. You're too tidy to be a boy, at least, a normal boy. I thought I'd leave you and that you'd get around to telling someone what the problem was."

"You'll tell Belindros? A girl can't be a Medici."

Marta stood and shook her head, "Take the bandages. If you need any help then come to me. Although you've managed very well so far."

Mika was stunned at her calm acceptance, "You're not going to throw me out?"

Marta laughed again, "It's no one's business but yours and besides, Lin would throw a fit if someone threw out his favourite apprentice." She opened the door and left Mika staring after her. Belindros' favourite apprentice? She walked slowly back to her room, deep in thought.

Having dressed properly, Mika grabbed Jon as he came downstairs and braced herself for his reaction. "Come on, let's get some reading done before breakfast." He started to protest through his yawns. "Two pages before you eat and I want your attention this time." He sulked his way through the two pages and Mika let him go to eat.

"Problems?"

Mika sighed at Marta's question, "I know he's bright, I know he can do this. I just don't know how to get him to do the things he doesn't like doing."

"He's been out at night again."

"I know. It's trying to keep him in that's the problem, he just climbs onto the roof if I tell him to stay in his room."

Mika rubbed her eyes. She'd thought Jon would be easier than Orai. Every time she told him off, he'd assure her with wide eyes that he'd do better. He did mean it, other things happened and he'd conveniently put his promises to one side. He could memorise by rote easily, getting him to do it was another matter. He couldn't understand why maths was important, history was worse. The thing was, she didn't have the time to watch him constantly. As he didn't have the skills to join in with the other boys, he normally helped with Marta in the kitchen during the day. It was a chore he was delighted with.

"I think you need to clamp down on him. Put him in with the other boys."

"He can't read or write properly yet, he won't manage."

Marta was firm, "It will either make him work to catch up or he will go under. If he goes under, then you'll have to make the decision whether to keep him or not."

Mika straightened, she was right, this couldn't go on forever. She walked into the kitchen, Jon was chortling over an unsuitable tale one of the guardsmen was telling, nearly choking on the food he stuffed into his mouth.

"Jon." At her tone he looked up, wary. "You'll be going in with the other boys from today."

Gavin caught on with a smile, "I'll take him up, make sure he doesn't get lost on the way there."

Jon's jaw dropped and he swallowed hastily, "It's a bit short notice, can't I go tomorrow?"

"No and you'll stop going out at night. During the evenings you can study with me. You'll need it to catch up."

At his protests, Mika gritted her teeth and pointed out he'd said that thumping a child for not learning was quite acceptable. Gavin sat next to them and described Mika's beating of Orai in his broadest possible terms. Jon's eyes grew wide and with the most innocent of faces, made a promise to do his best. Mika rolled her own eyes, at least until the next time he was distracted.

An apprentice came to find her while she helped Enos that morning to say she was wanted by Varian. Enos looked pained, then shrugged and told her to go. She found him in a small room tucked into the depths of the hospice. Varian was an old sharp faced man, with the hairiest arms Mika had ever seen. She was informed that he expected her to be with him at the same time every week.

She sat with another apprentice and a journeyman she vaguely knew. Given a sheet of paper and a pen, she was told to make notes while Varian interviewed the returning Medici. Mika had been aware of the constant stream of Medici coming in and out of the hospice, Belindros wasn't the only one that travelled and an overview of the country could be gathered from the all the information they gathered. Reports of disease and new cures were dismissed or written down for experimentation.

Varian was a hard taskmaster and without Belindros' saving grace of wit. The apprentices were expected to discuss the details afterwards and make intelligent comments. Mika was behind most of the others, she'd not even heard of some of these countries or their histories with Ackbarr. No allowances were made and she came out frustrated at her lack of knowledge. As Varian had said, his dark shaven face stony, she would be expected to make all sorts of decisions as a Medici, sometimes with only half the facts and she needed to learn to use her brain.

Jon also came back that afternoon sour faced and sulky. The other boys had looked down on him, teasing him over his size and lack of learning. The tutors had leant on him to produce the required standard. Any enquires brought out a vile level of language from him.

Mika held her breath and watched as he sat in the study that evening and stared blankly at his book, holding his pencil in a tight fist as he tried to work through the problems set. She told him that she'd expect him to continue his reading with her in the morning and nearly ducked as his arm twitched. She got her own books out and studied alongside him, despite the afternoon with Varian having given her a headache.

"How is your ferret getting on?"

Mika was watching Belindros make up an order. "Better than Orai," she hedged.

He snorted, she knew he'd be keeping abreast of the situation. If it didn't work out, then he'd be the first to say and expect her to deal with it. "I'd stew your ferret, only there's not enough meat on him to make a meal." She relaxed, not yet then. He changed the subject, "Look these up while I mix them boy and tell me what you think."

"Can't I help?"

"Not with this, the book's on the desk. Thimal, look it up."

She obediently found the correct herb and read out the properties. "How are they going to be used?"

"These ones are for steeping in hot water, the patient drinks it." Belindros explained, "The Sweetroot is for smoking. Here, smell." It was an aniseed smell, sweetly potent. He watched her carefully as she flinched away.

She read, "Sweetroot, causes dulling of the senses, befuddlement in small doses, to be used carefully in cases of delirium." Mika peered over, curious at the amount in the pan. "How much are you using per dose?" He showed her and she checked the book, "That's twice the amount recommended, you could drop a horse with that much!"

"My, aren't we the expert? My client has been using it a while, he needs a lot these days." His face was impassive, "I'd use Corettle but he refuses to go near it..." He rubbed his eyes into the crook of his elbow, carefully keeping his face away from the herbs.

"Who is the client?"

"Never you mind. Someone important. However, if I drop dead tomorrow, the ingredients are on that list there. The ingredients and quantities are not to be meddled with." The drugs were packed into a small box and sealed with Belindros' personal seal. "I will deliver them later and no, you are not coming with me."

Belindros had left to deliver his order. She wondered vaguely who it was while she attempted to continue Jon's lessons. Most people collected their own prescriptions. Jon was restless, looking out of the window and fidgeting.

"Jon, Belindros was asking about you. I need you to behave, to learn." Mika's frustration boiled over. Jon muttered into his shirt and she was reminded of her own reactions to her mother's nagging. She swallowed her guilt and tried again, "I know you can do all these things, you need to show the masters as well."

He looked rebellious, "They sit there and ignore the other boys messing around, then when I do something wrong, they yell at me."

"Do you give them cause to yell?"

Jon shrugged, twisting himself into a knot. "They think I'm stupid."

"You remember the things I tell you. You're far better than Orai." She thought a while, "I think you need to come with me to the hospice tomorrow, the other apprentices have their boys there. You should be there too."

"Do you get yelled at?"

"Not yelled at, but Varian isn't nice. Anything I say or write has to be just so." She thought hard, "Maybe in a way it's good. I need to be sure of what I'm doing, make educated guesses, not just blurt things out under pressure. And I will be under pressure at some point. I need to be able to think. So maybe, he's doing me a favour." She still wasn't sure, although Jon looked impressed with her explanation. Privately she thought Varian was just a nasty old man who'd taken a dislike to her.

Chapter 14

Jon pointed out, "Your hair, it's not as light as I thought it was. It's gone dark at the roots." Mika swore and took out the package given to her by the barber. She mixed it in a small bowl as he'd told her. Jon watched, looking sceptical and commented on the disgusting smell.

"Can you help? I can't see." They were sitting in the courtyard and for once it was quiet. Jon recoiled, pulling a face. Squeamishly, he dabbed at her head, making rude remarks about his eyes stinging. A competent set of hands took over, she glanced up and quickly shut her own eyes as they began to stream. Marta had pushed Jon to one side.

"There, you'll need to stay in the sun for a bit. Scrub the mud off these for me while you wait. There's the sand timer, wash the bleach off when it's finished."

Relieved, Mika sat in the sun and washed the vegetables, in between smacking Jon's hands as he stole them to toss into his mouth. After she'd rinsed the bleach off, her head tingled and Jon pulled faces at the smell until she threatened to dunk him.

"You've gone blond again boy." Belindros made the comment halfway through her session with him. She shrugged in what she hoped was a boyish manner. He grunted and lost interest, "Well, it's probably for the best. You'll be attending me at the palace this evening. Best robes tonight boy."

Mika wore her best set of clothes with delight. The long Medici apprentice robes suited her height and disguised her figure further. She gazed around the palace as they entered, trying to keep an eye on where they were going at the same time. Belindros lectured her on etiquette while they walked. She was to serve him in certain ways, to watch and imitate the other boys. She got the impression he didn't enjoy the palace dinners and wondered why.

She'd not been inside the fortress before, the apprentices were kept in the hospice unless they had a reason for going elsewhere. The entrance was built to impress, narrow staircases leading upwards into the gloom and smoky flares adding to the smell of people. The great hall was truly enormous, a fireplace at each end, tapestries showing battle scenes and long tables with places set ready for the guests.

Belindros moved to an area close to one end. A servant intercepted him and showed him to a place. She was motioned to stand behind Belindros' chair, ready to help serve him the titbits he preferred. Other boys stood behind their masters waiting to help in the same way. The hall filled rapidly, nobles and their pages being shown where to sit. The murmur of conversation didn't quite fill the echoing space.

She started as Belindros stood, others were standing and looking towards the dais. A movement in the gloom and a man came out, in middle years, swarthy in the Ackbarr way and Mika realised she was looking at the King. This was the man who threatened her country. Not large, he had a calm face under his beard. He didn't look like an aggressor. She noticed the nobles bowing, the pages kneeling and made to copy when a hand came under her arm. She looked at Belindros and he shook his head.

"Medici," came the quiet comment. She wasn't expected to kneel. Uncomfortable with standing while others knelt, she inclined her head as a gesture of respect and was relieved when the nobles began to sit. The conversation bubbled up again as servants began passing around platters and wine.

Mika stared around the dark hall. The King sat high on the dais. Others made quiet conversation to him, bending their heads and flattering. He was not young, but there was a younger woman sitting close by and few spoke to her. Mika felt for her, remembering her time at her wedding, sitting there with people staring. She wondered if that was his oldest daughter or his new wife and couldn't tell, it could be either. She took a pitcher from a passing servant and filled Belindros' cup.

She blinked as she spotted the man from the menagerie. Jace, the King's Advisor for War was sprawled in his chair, close to the King. She wondered where the cat was. A space was around him as the smoke curled out of his mouth, a cylinder of herbs held lazily between two fingers. Conversation was muted in that corner. Every so often the King would lean down and make a remark and the man would reply, smiling.

Belindros muttered a comment and she picked up several tiny sweetmeats for him from the serving boy. She sniffed, certain she could smell the tang of Sweetroot over the smell of food. This must have been who the order was for. Jace was relaxed, his eyes half closed. He was handsome. As dark blond as she'd been before she'd bleached her hair, the cheekbones and long eyes were unmistakable as Cassai. She had a nagging sense of knowing him and tried to work out who he reminded her of. With a shock she realised it was her mother.

Unsettled, she gazed elsewhere, further down the table and nearly dumped the contents of the plate she held into Belindros' lap. It was her father in his full court regalia. Looking at the pale hair against the dark sober clothing, she felt her heart thump in longing. A whispered acerbic comment came from Belindros, wanting to know why he wasn't getting his food. She ducked her head, paying attention to his wishes and minded him, not wanting her father to notice her.

There was a pause between the servings. An announcement came from a portly man whose deep chest flung his words across the hall. The diners hushed in anticipation and Mika was reminded of the crowd in the menagerie.

A man was ushered in between two large guards. Mika wasn't listening to the words from the steward, out of habit from Belindros' teachings, she was watching the man's face and clothes. He was bull-like and strong and he bellowed back at the accusations, his accent so thick it was difficult to understand what he was defying. The King leaned down to Jace, murmured a few words. A question? Jace smiled in return, a sleepy twitch of his lips. He carefully blew the last of the smoke out of his mouth and placed the Sweetroot ashes on his plate. Tension in the hall rose as he stood.

The steward announced into the silence, "You have your choice, die now or fight with the chance to live." Mika saw Jace through the man's eyes, a similar height, but not as wide, not as strong. She wanted to cry out to warn him, she'd seen the way he moved in the menagerie. The man nodded, his eyes eager and he accepted the sword when his hands were untied.

Jace's movements were languid, an inevitable deadliness gathering, like thick honey dripping off a spoon. He dipped his head to the King and stepped forwards into the space between the tables. The man lunged and Jace shifted sideways out of reach. Another lunge, the sword flicking to the side. The condemned man was good, Mika could recognise that from her own training. Gavin could've despatched him, but Jace hadn't even drawn his sword yet. Jace moved again, looking sleepily amused. Mika watched with a growing horror, if this was what he was like drugged with Sweetroot, then what could he achieve with a clear head?

The man paused as Jace finally drew his sword and a mad hope came into his eyes. Mika was frozen to the spot, her mouth dry. Couldn't he see that he was being played with? His tunic was soaked in sweat, his breathing harsh in the silent room. With no other choice he thrust again and slashed, in a frenzy that went nowhere. Jace was fast, his muscles shifting smoothly to block the attack. Mika flinched from the echoes in the hall, blinked as Jace's sword flicked out and the man stood still, disbelief on his face.

Jace turned his back and twitched a napkin from one of the diners, wiped his sword and walked away. The man gazed down at his stomach, dropping his own sword as he clutched at the red line seeping through his clothes. Too shocked to speak, his mouth gaped as he slowly crumpled onto the floor. Mika felt sick. It had all been a show. The King proving his point that he had the deadliest swordsman with him.

Without meaning to, she glanced at her father, his face had twisted in disgust as he looked at Jace, now sprawled back in his chair. Jace winked back at him, an unexpected mischief in his face, aware there was nothing her father could do. They were of a similar age, Jace and her father, both in their early thirties. The differences were clear, her father was an ambassador of a small country here under sufferance, a country with goods Ackbarr wanted and Jace under the King's protection used for his skills.

The dinner continued as the mess in the middle of the floor was cleared up. The nobles ignored it, Mika had the feeling it was an often repeated show. Belindros ate little and she suspected that he was as disgusted as she was. He guarded his usually acerbic tongue and was charming to the nobles on either side of him, exchanging tales of the countries and people they had in common.

The feasting carried on late into the night. Belindros motioned for her to leave at the earliest possible time. Many still sat hoping for more wine, more food and more entertainment. She tucked Belindros' cloak around him and followed behind, deep in thought, nearly stumbling into him as he stopped in the corridor.

"Ambassador Koren."

Mika jumped, forgetting to keep her head down as she gazed into her father's eyes. The blood drained out of his face and she remembered seeing her brother's face in the mirror the day she'd cut her hair. Unable to think, she automatically gave the traditional bow a Cassai youngster gave to an elder.

"This is Mikon, my apprentice. Mikon, I believe you said your mother was Cassai?" Belindros' voice was crisp. She peeped upwards, her father was staring at Belindros, mouth slightly open.

"Yes." Her voice was barely a whisper.

Other people were passing them, staring in curiosity. Her father coughed and recovered himself. He nodded, his face his usual mask, only his eyes showing his confusion. Mika flicked her eyes towards the servant behind him, thankfully he wasn't one she recognised.

"It is a beautiful night, I intend to enjoy it Ambassador. I take it you feel the same." Belindros was covering for him.

"Yes. Good night Medici." Her father bowed to Belindros and left, his back taut.

Belindros glanced at her, "Come on boy, back home. I tire easily these days."

Jon wasn't in his bed when she got back. Mika muttered a rude word and made a note to tell him off when she saw him in the morning, she couldn't think straight at the moment.

She came downstairs yawning the next morning, plonked herself down on the bench and took the bread and jam offered by one of the servants.

"Is Jon not up yet?"

Mika looked at Marta, stirring a pot on the stove, "I looked in last night, he wasn't in his room. Haven't you seen him?"

Marta shook her head, "Not like Jon to miss a meal." Mika stuffed the rest of her bread in her mouth and ran back up the stairs to look. The bed was in the same state. She walked slowly down.

"He didn't sleep in his bed last night."

"He didn't mention anything to me." Gavin looked concerned. For all his teasing, Gavin had developed a fondness for Jon.

Marta offered her opinion, "He may have decided it's all too much. He'll turn up."

Mika shook her head, she couldn't believe Jon would just disappear. She floundered through the tiredness from the previous evening, "I need to look for him."

"If he doesn't want to be found then he won't be. He'll be back at some point. He's a street child and you have your lessons to go to."

Mika opened her mouth to protest when Gavin spoke up, "I'll take a look around the markets, see if anyone's seen him."

Mika walked to the palace in a daze. No Jon. No constant chatter distracting her. She waved at the familiar guards on the gates, barely registering them. She was kept busy at the hospice. Autumn had come to Ackbarr and coughs and colds had arrived with it. She scarcely had the time to think about what she did, let alone think about the look in her father's eyes. Her father was here. She'd dreamt of finding him in Ackbarr, not dared to hope she would. She jumped back into reality, catching a small child who nearly wriggled off the examining table.

Gavin came back with bad news that evening, he'd not found any sign of Jon. She stared at Jon's empty room. All his things still there, she paused. All his things, he wouldn't have left food. The bottled preserves were still on the shelf. Jon had a weakness for them and would beg extra from Marta in return for good behaviour. Jon would have taken those bottles with him, no way would he have left them.

She remembered a man sitting by the gate to the compound yesterday and Jon looking everywhere but in his direction. He'd rushed into the compound, dragging her in behind him. The man had appeared drunk. She'd not looked twice, despite people not normally sitting in the streets here. Her suspicions rose, she was positive Jon hadn't gone voluntarily.

She wandered downstairs, "Marta, do you know where Jon lived with his mother?"

"Yes, on the east side, close to the gates. You'll have to ask around."

Gavin came in having heard the last comment, his eyes looking for food. The big man seemed to have a stomach as bottomless as Jon's. "What was his father's name?" Mika shrugged, he'd talked as little as possible about his father and home life.

"Hanion." Marta supplied, "He's not pleasant."

"Let's look then. Unpleasant I can deal with," Gavin said rubbing his knuckles.

Chapter 15

This part of Ackbarr Mika had only explored with Jon briefly. It was the first area she'd seen that was overcrowded and insanitary. Washing hung from the windows. Small and not so small boys peeing on the street corners. Even the streets felt cramped here, eyes watching them from dark doorways. It reminded her of the forest back in Cassai, danger lurking behind every corner. Responding without realising, Mika began to walk on her toes, a smoothness in her gait, unaware her nostrils were flaring, breathing in the multitude of rank smells.

Dusk dimmed the alleyways further as they ducked into taverns, asking about Jon's father. She got the feeling people didn't want to talk, whether just to her or whether it was Hanion's reputation, she wasn't sure. Her features were glanced at slyly from the corner of eyes. She'd worn her Medici robes, giving her a grudging respect from the traders.

Gavin's huge presence behind helped to bolster her courage. She was unaware it was the slender Cassai youth they watched, not Gavin. The look in her eye demanding respect from those further down the food chain. Gavin noticed and remained silent. Long years of working with Belindros had taught him when to keep his mouth shut and when to use his bulk to persuade matters.

They quickly became frustrated, days passed as they walked through the streets every evening, seeing large families crammed into small rooms. Dirty alleys where whores shrieked at being disturbed, their customers shifting away, faces averted, fingers fumbling at the ties to their trousers. Finally they found Hanion.

A tavern they'd been in before, the barman recognised them and nodded towards a tall raw boned man sitting in the corner. Gavin loomed his way, blocking the exit. Mika dragged a stool over to sit opposite him, trying not to breathe in the rank sweat and bad breath. Something inside her recoiled, she disliked this place, this man, her eyes grew colder. Hanion played it cool, his hand only trembling slightly as he drank from the clay cup and stared back.

"You're Hanion."

"May be."

Gavin leant over and knocked the cup from his hand. "Answer him." It smashed in the suddenly quiet room.

He looked sulky as the barman turned his face away. Gavin was twice the size of any man there and had the look of being able to use the sword strapped to his side. "Yes."

Mika led the interrogation, "Where's Jon?"

"What does it matter to you?"

"Answer me."

"Jon happens to be my son. I have the use of him until he's thirteen and apprenticed to the man of my choice."

"Jon is a member of Belindros the Medici's household."

He grinned, showing blackened teeth, "Tough titty boy, he's mine." She was struck that Jon didn't look much like his father. Dislike for the man swept over her.

She bluffed, "Tell me or I'll dislocate every bone in your body."

"You're an apprentice Medici. You harm me and I can have you expelled boy." Her hopes plummeted.

"He can be expelled, I can't be." Gavin's voice was quiet. "Mikon, step outside for a bit and get some fresh air, will you? I'm sure Belindros wouldn't like you to get involved in anything nasty."

Gavin dragged Hanion upright and Mika pushed her stool away feeling sick. There was nothing she could do, no other way to get Hanion to talk. She turned, seeing the group of men standing behind them watching the show. Their eyes were hostile, glaring. She winced and realised the mood was directed at Hanion, he wasn't liked and the atmosphere had turned ugly with the expectation of a fight. Mika wished she'd brought her rapier. She squared her shoulders and the crowd parted to let her out.

"City guard coming by." The warning was low, enough to carry within the room, not to the outside. Gavin swore and shoved Hanion backwards into the wall, no time to try anything.

"Too late big man." Hanion had managed to keep his smirk, although by now it looked in a rictus. Gavin knotted his fists, controlling his urge to pummel this man into the ground. Hanion slid out of the tavern as the city guard walked by.

"We won't find him again." Gavin's voice was matter of fact.

"What shall we do?"

Gavin shrugged, "Keep looking, someone will talk. They don't like him."

A week passed, the lessons failed to keep her attention while she worried. She was reprimanded gently several times at the hospice by Abran. Varian as sharp tempered as ever, gave her no quarter, insisting she concentrated and piled yet more work onto her. Enos asked her about Jon and looked surprised when she said he'd gone missing. His offer to ask his family to keep an eye out for Jon touched her, despite knowing they wouldn't find a street child amongst the hundreds. The rumours spread quickly, Orai hadn't been taken on by another apprentice yet. He slyly tried his best to ingratiate himself with her and began to cause trouble when she refused his advances.

Belindros called her into his office close to the end of the week. Mika went, expecting to be told off for her lack of concentration. He surprised her by asking about Jon and listened to her concerns. She told him about the meeting with Jon's father. Belindros nodded and said he'd ask the journeymen Medici to make enquires. Working down in the city, they heard many things others didn't.

Her dreams echoed her frustration. She frequently woke in the night, sweating and shaking. Disturbed by their intensity, she struggled to contain her subconscious wish to rend, to taste the iron sweetness as she sank her teeth into prey and shake it into submission.

Mika came back after lessons to discover the compound in a bustle. Belindros had just got off his horse, Gavin's was being led to the stables. Guards and servants stood around, talking.

"He's in there boy." Belindros waved a hand and stalked off to his rooms. Mika rushed into the bathhouse. Jon had been stripped by Gavin and dunked in the tub. Marta came in behind her with an armful of towels and clothes.

Mika barely recognised him, Jon had never been big, but now he looked half starved, his limbs mottled with bruising and he was curled up in the tub shaking. His head had been shaved, taking away his identity. Gavin sat next to Jon, talking soothingly, splashing warm water over him. Jon clung to her hand when she gave it to him.

"Someone talked." Gavin's voice was quiet. "I found him at the docks and sent Amos for Belindros." She nodded. Jon didn't look like he was listening, his eyes were glazed and his body shifting passively under Gavin's big hands.

Gavin dried Jon and carried him upstairs, wrapping his blankets around him. Mika sat with him, helping him to eat, several of his teeth were loose. The story came out in odd muddles, none in the right order.

"I'd met Da a few times, he was always asking for money, for drinking."

"What money did you give him?" She guessed he'd given something to Hanion.

"My allowance." He sniffed and Mika's anger grew. Jon didn't get much, only enough for sweets and the occasional treat.

"He asked me to steal things from here, said a Medici would never miss it… I said I wouldn't do it… It was supposed to be the last time we'd met. I'd refused to take any more money, he hit me. I tried to run, but someone tripped me up." A child's indignation over the unfairness. He'd been grabbed on his way out. "He wouldn't let me go."

Gavin came up to relieve Mika so she could eat and Jon was still mumbling through his experiences when she returned. Gavin's eyes were flat with anger and although his voice and hands were gentle with Jon, she didn't think much of Hanion's chances if their paths crossed again.

"He tied me up, I tried to promise to steal things. To get away." He looked earnestly up at Mika and she nodded her approval. "He wouldn't believe me. He came in drunk one evening and started yelling about how people were talking about me. He said there was only one place for me now."

Mika hugged him. "You should have told me. No more secrets Jon." He agreed, shivering, looking even smaller in his blankets with no hair. He fell asleep, still muttering.

Mika heard about the rescue from Gavin later, when Jon had fallen asleep deeply enough for her to leave him.

"You should have seen him." Gavin was chortling as he referred to Belindros, "Sat on his horse, staring down his nose in the way he does best." Mika was too relieved about finding Jon to join in the laughter at the long table. They'd found Jon at the docks, waiting to be transported further downstream. The man had protested he was going to be apprenticed as a sailor. Gavin snorted at this, it was well known that boys were sold for the whorehouses or as slaves. Belindros had claimed him for his household and paid the apprentice fee to the river man. Jon was officially Belindros' for the next five years.

Jon spent several days looking subdued and took a while to regain his cheerful nature. Gavin walked him to the palace and back each day, Jon had insisted he go. Mika was surprised by his determination to learn. He attacked his studies with a fierceness, refusing to be beaten.

"I'm not going back there," was all he would say. Mika's heart bled for him, there was no way she would ever let him go back.

Mika went to thank Belindros. He refused to accept her thanks saying gruffly, "I knew his mother, she was a lovely lady." His eyebrows were down, his face glowering as he changed the subject, "Lanen, find it and tell me it's properties." Mika knew better than to ask more. Belindros stayed out of her way for the next few days, insisting she help in the hospice.

Now they'd found Jon and he was safe, Mika went out with the others in her group in the evenings to let off steam from the tests with her tutors. Not feeling the cool air, they larked about, jumping off walls and benches in the ornamental parks and scaring lovers in secluded corners with delight.

Mika and Lissina watched the others race ahead, Jenna picked up her skirts and raced with the boys, laughing at their teasing. Lissina squealed and held onto Mika's arm as a shadow separated itself from the trees. Mika felt it was a little contrived, Lissina had been using any excuse recently, even changing her desk with Jenna to be closer to her. She wasn't sure how she felt about it, she liked Lissina, but not in the way Lissina wanted.

The shadow cleared and Jace stared coolly at them. It was the first time she'd seen him close up. Again, she noticed the striking resemblance to her mother, the dark sandy hair and green eyes, the freckles across his nose. His eyes flickered to Mika and became startled before returning to boredom. She could feel a magnetism flowing between them, creating an attraction that tugged at her.

Jace inclined his head to Lissina, who flushed and clutched Mika's arm tighter as he walked away with an easy stride. Another shadow detached itself from the trees and loped after him.

Lissina sighed. "I would love to stroke that cat. Is that something all Cassai can do?"

Mika shook her head, "It shouldn't be here."

She was pushed teasingly, "You're a romantic. It was roaming the countryside killing things before he caught it. It's well fed now, happy."

"It should be in Cassai, hunting small creatures in the forest." Her feelings plummeted, there was something wrong about a wild creature following Jace around like that. In a foul mood she ignored the others returning and Lissina chattering about Jace and his attentions.

While sorting through dirty equipment in the examination rooms, she asked Belindros about Jace.

"That's the King's Advisor, stay away from him. He eats children like you for breakfast." For once he looked serious. "His habits are not pleasant and I've had to deal with the fallout on many occasions, so stay away"

"What do you mean?"

"There are rumours about him, rumours I choose to believe. The royal family is cursed in your land. If they inbreed too much, something happens, a changing." Mika went cold and tried scoffing. Belindros was serious, "No, I believe this." He was speaking quietly, his eyes on the corridor in front of them, watching the open door. "I have had to deal with the consequences of Jace's appetites. A cat's penis has barbs it on you know, that's why a female cat screams during intercourse."

Belindros' face was in its most clinical expression, Mika's insides went liquid at the thought.

"I have also read the historical accounts from your land Mikon, as a Medici I have access to much information. I believe Jace has control of his gift and can change at will."

"I saw Jace inside the cat cage at the menagerie. They didn't attack him."

"The dominant male is supposed to be able to control others of their kind, to force them to change and he can smell when the females are on heat. It makes him uncontrollable. Thankfully there is only Jace, any others have been exterminated by your people. Only the women breed true and they have always been few and far between. There are more males born, but they cannot breed true changers, not like the females. There is only one woman currently alive that might be suitable, but she is married to a powerful man. Jace cannot touch her."

His voice was quietly angry, urgent. "That is the real reason why the King wants your land completely subjugated. It's not the timber or the plants in your forests. Excuses, all of them. He wants to breed killers, killers controlled only by him. I have heard the King has dreams of owning an army of men that is fearless and unstoppable. While Jace continues to be useful, the King will protect him from those wanting their revenge for his actions. The King is only lacking in support from his nobles for his vision of destroying Cassai. He feeds their basest appetites with those shows during the feasts he gives. When he has their blood lust roused, then he will lead them over your mountains."

Mika remembered the high passes she'd travelled through to Fenin and saw in her mind thousands of men pouring down into the forests of her sparsely populated country. She shook the thought out of her mind. "How did he come to be here?"

"Jace escaped your country when he was about your age." He watched her carefully as he spoke. "The rumours are that he narrowly escaped being gelded."

"They don't do things like that in my country!" She snapped back unthinking.

"He raped a woman from the royal family. There are many things you don't hear boy, so stay away from him."

They finished quietly, Mika no longer wanting to talk.

Mika locked her door, sweating. She'd been having the dreams again. They'd been coming through stronger since she'd met Jace. She'd seen him several times, watching her with a puzzled look on his face, that quickly changed to an insolent stare when anyone noticed. She'd tried not to notice him, copied his coolness if he met her gaze and messed around with the rest of her class, shoving and laughing. But every time she saw him, she felt vulnerable and she got the feeling he was curious too, trying to work something out.

That tugging between them, she remembered Belindros' words that he would be able to control others like him. Was this what she was? Had she changed at Fenin? She spent the day fretting over everything that had happened, turning it over in her mind until she'd felt sick with a pounding headache, unable to eat much at dinner. She had to find out if it was true and learn to control it.

The household was empty, Belindros had collected everyone up to go to a concert. She'd pleaded a headache. She'd wanted to go, but this was more important, she had to try this while everyone as out, otherwise she might end up with everyone dead around her again.

She sat on the bed and thought about her dreams. Closing her eyes she concentrated, the forest felt far away from here. Minutes passed and nothing happened. Two dimensional trees flickered in front of her closed eyes, echoes of animals distorted by distance. Thoughts of the day kept intruding, Jon's shrill laugh, the way he folded up at Gavin's teasing. The smell of dinner in the kitchen, firelight, reflections in puddles.

Frustrated, Mika stripped off and lay down. Trying to conjure up the sensations and the feelings she'd had in Fenin. A streak of anger ran through at her inability to summon this changing. That it happened of its own accord, beyond her control and as she thought of Jace's mocking eyes part of her stirred. Her skin twitched as though something lay beneath. Sweat trickled down her back. The room was stuffy with the shutters closed. She didn't want to be in here, she wanted to be outside, in the cool air, stalking. The eyes grew larger in her mind, she whimpered and stretched. Anger, why was she trapped here? She encouraged it, focussing on the eyes, tickling the sensation. Her mouth yawned and kept yawning. Twisting back, she arched on the bed, joints popping as they changed direction. Unable to cry out, she writhed and remembered nothing until the morning.

Mika woke to find the room wrecked. Cold and shaking, she gazed at the claw marks on the walls, deep wide gouges that could never have been made by her fingers. The blankets were shredded and covered in fine pale hairs. The room stank and she ached. It was true.

She covered her face, she'd killed Rylan, she was the murderer. She forced herself to breathe deeply, holding back the hysterics that threatened to take hold.

Relief made her weak as she noticed her door was still locked. She lay stiff on the bed, the moments endless as she listened for noises, desperate for some form of normality. She heard someone moving around downstairs and Gavin's voice out in the yard and slumped with her hands over her eyes.

A knock on the door and she jumped as Jon shouted, "Breakfast's ready, how's your head?" He was used to her keeping him out, but he was full of the evening concert, wanting to explain the sounds that had filled him. He slid in while she was distractedly tying her shirt laces and his jaw dropped. "What happened in here?"

"You mustn't say anything."

"Sure." He looked puzzled, "So, what are all these scrapes from?"

"I don't know, I'm not sure." She held her head while she tried to think. "Look, can you get me outside the walls for the night?"

"There's a postern gate in the south wall, I know some of the guards." He touched the wall, "Marta's going to kill you if she sees this. These look like claw marks..."

"Yes. Can you introduce me to the guards you know?"

"Can I come too?"

"No. It's not safe."

"Then I'm not doing anything until you've told me." He crossed his arms and looked stubborn, ignoring her glower. "No secrets remember?" The bell rang for breakfast and he raced downstairs with a grin, knowing it would be the last chance she'd have to speak with him alone until the evening.

That day took ages. She was distracted and had to be reprimanded by Abran several times for not paying attention. The other students teased her, assuming her distraction was due to a girl. Lissina pouted but even their comments failed to shake her out of her thoughts.

Jon and Mika sat high on the old city walls, the evening wind had an edge, a sharp reminder of the coming winter. Shouts filtered up from the dockside far below. Jon sat next to her, munching on his pie. "Come on then, no secrets?"

She checked the area around them. Couples walked past and there was no one close by. "I'm a girl."

His jaw dropped, "You're kidding me." She flushed as he looked her up and down, "You've not got any..." His hands sketched out where her breasts should be.

"You're too young to notice things like that."

He grinned, shaking his head, "Do you remember Drutha's?" Mika nodded, even she'd heard of the biggest whore house in Ackbarr. "I used to run errands for her, the things I've seen there." He pretended to lean back with a faraway look in his eye, a man of the world. She poked him in the ribs and he collapsed, chortling, into the small skinny boy he was.

"Why do you think I've been keeping you out of my room?"

Jon shrugged, settling the new information into his mind. "So," He was all practicality now, "Claw marks on the walls aren't normal, even at Drutha's." He assumed a calculating expression, "I think you have to pay extra for that."

"Thanks, if I ever need a new career I'll remember. Jon, what do you know about Jace, the King's Advisor for War?"

"Stay away from him. Nasty. Rumours about..." He stopped and eyed her, suddenly wary.

"I think I'm the same, I changed last night. Jon, I need your help to get past the city walls after dark. I need to learn how to control this. I've not got any time during the day and I don't want to hurt anyone else."

His sharp mind caught the extra word, "What do you mean anyone else?"

She put her head in her hands, "I killed my husband." Quietly, tears began to fill her eyes and she wiped them away, knowing she had to continue appearing a boy.

He stared, stunned into silence, then nodded. "I'll sort something. It might take a while."

Chapter 16

To her frustration, Mika was unable to practice that evening. Belindros had arranged to have the musicians play at his house, a privilege of being Medici. Guests had been invited and Mika was expected to attend and be sociable. Jon tugged at her arm in excitement, desperate for a repeat of the previous evening. Mika wanted to brood at the back over her problems and was foiled by the music. Her mind spun away with her, held down only by Jon unconsciously gripping her hand, transported in his own reverie.

Her eyes wandered over the musicians and was caught by the gitern player. He was large, his thick fingers delicately placed themselves on the strings. He seemed to play without thought, his eyes flicking over those listening, so sure of his own ability. Mika was struck by the difference between his face, that of a ruffian and his fingers dancing, playing like an angel. In the split second before his eyes moved to her, she remembered – she was a boy. She switched her face into the cool stare she used for Jace and his gaze passed over her.

The countryside around Ackbarr was very different from the landscapes she dreamed of. Wide open spaces and the large river winding its way to the plains below the mountains. She twitched as an owl hooted and the grasses rustled around her. Jon had agreed to be left behind, on condition of her telling him everything.

She and Jon had sneaked out of the house and joined the few people darting through the streets. There were patrols to keep order in the dark night. They easily avoided them, Jon grinning with excitement. Mika concentrated on the way through the city, she didn't want to get lost on her way back. Jon was greeted by the guards at the gate with pleasure and he introduced Mika as a friend. Bored of standing at the closed gate for several hours, the guards welcomed the diversion and talked eagerly. A few coins were exchanged, a signal arranged so she could get back in and then she was outside, with the gate closing behind her.

Mika was unsettled by the wide views, unable to relax. Something inside made her want enclosed spaces, somewhere to hide. She found a small copse away from the gate and sat for a while, staring at the larger of the two moons, trying to relax. Night noises distracted her, different from her dreams, adding to her isolation.

Jon had been fascinated, telling her about the rumours of Jace. They unsettled her more than anything, she knew they weren't rumours. That thing that tugged her, pulled her towards him, Jace must realise there was something about her, it must affect him too. The only thing stopping him was that he didn't think she was a girl or part of the royal family. Her mother's blood, it must have come through her mother. Her mother rarely visited her family and always on her own. Mika had never been allowed to see them, only from a distance with the rest of the population. Jace would have come from the same part of the family, were he and her mother cousins? She'd certainly never met him. He must have left years ago.

Abruptly she remembered, if she changed then she'd have no clothes left. She swore at the thought of trying to get home in rags. Shivering in the chilly night air, she stripped, made a bag out of her tunic and hung it on a branch. Being naked made her feel vulnerable, more aware of not belonging in the dark. She spent several hours trying to change and failed utterly. The large moon set and she tramped back to bed by the pale light of the smaller one.

Jon was bouncing the next day, knocking on her door and asking questions. Mika held her head and muttered her answers. He was cheerful, assuring her that it would happen at some point. Mika wasn't so sure.

Mika had noticed the trader with herbs and spices on her stall in the square at other points when she'd passed through on her way to the palace. Belindros had waved his disdain, there was nothing there suitable for his line of work. However she still sniffed in appreciation as she went by. She loved the scents, those for cooking or for strewing in chests to keep clothes fresh and moth free.

Coming closer she noticed a familiar bundle of small dried flowers. Her breath caught, they were vineflowers, her mother's favourite. Shyly she asked the trader about them. The trader shrugged, she couldn't sell them, nobody liked the scent. It was too strange for Ackbarr, she wouldn't be buying them again. Mika asked how much and delighted, paid over the amount asked, telling the trader she had a customer if she could get more. She showed them to Jon, who spluttered his disgust.

In her rooms that evening, she sewed several small sachets to put her vineflowers in. She pressed them against her mouth and nose, breathing in the peppery citrus smell. She tucked them into her chest between her clothes and giggled over Marta sniffing the air. Marta rarely came up to her rooms. After the first few weeks of checking that things were kept tidy, she'd stopped, expecting Mika to deal with everything herself.

Abran turned to Jon and asked him to get the Volos. Jon looked panicked. Mika swiftly intervened as Jon took a breath to give his usual smart reply for when he didn't know an answer. "Jon, up the corridor, fourth turning on the right..."

She gave the rest of the directions knowing Jon with his street child's brain would remember clearly. "The words on the jar look like this." She wrote them down on a scrap torn from her notebook. "It's a clear jar with a yellowish liquid in it." Jon took the paper and dashed off.

"Apologies Medici, Jon's reading still isn't perfect." The younger boys sniggered, led by Orai. Abran nodded calmly and they waited. Jon arrived in short order. Abran took the jar from him, smiled and continued his lecture as if nothing had happened. Mika exchanged grins with Jon, one up to them.

The trips to the hospice helped Jon's confidence. Mika continued his lessons in the evenings, memorising information with him in the early morning at breakfast and on their way to the hospice. His memory really was far better than hers, a lack of reading meant he'd learnt to remember. She'd read through her history before breakfast and give him the salient points and he could soon rattle them off. He came home delighted one afternoon while she'd been with her own tutor group.

"I did it!"

Gavin measured him with his hand, "Nope, still not grown." Jon pushed him away as they all laughed.

"What?"

Jon rarely looked this happy. "A tutor asked about the campaign in Sandros, none of the other boys knew much. I quoted the entire text at them. They had to look it up!" Mika cheered him, delighted. It was a turning point with the tutors beginning to appreciate his skills and he started to put more effort into reading and writing.

Mika was walking in the garden with Lissina before lessons. Her tall serious father had watched them go with a smile on his solemn face. Mika was in full flow as a boy now and had been accepted as part of the tutor group. It was sometimes difficult to remember that she was a girl, so used to the easy arrogant ways she copied. She'd been certain they'd notice in the beginning, but it appeared that they assumed any differences were due to her being foreign.

Despite her initial shyness, she'd formed good relationships with both the girls as well as the boys. The other boys could still be awkward around the girls, Mika laughed and teased them as much as they did her. Lissina especially would talk with her, Mika wished with all her heart she could tell her secret.

Lissina was in a careless mood, picking flowers and giving them to Mika to hold. She had yet another new set of dresses, complimenting her tiny figure, her mass of curly dark hair barely held back by the matching ribbon. Mika eyed it with a pang of envy, knowing she'd need to check her own roots again shortly. The air was balmy in the autumnal sunshine and the brief respite from lessons was fabulous.

"What will you do when you've become a Medici?"

Mika shrugged, "I don't know, travel maybe, see the world."

"You could stay here." Lissina stopped and gazed up at her. Mika felt awkward, there was an expectancy about Lissina and Mika wasn't sure what she wanted. Lissina sat down and patted the seat beside her.

Mika tried an explanation, "I want to learn the things the Medici can't teach me here and find out more by travelling. New Medici often travel, it's a good way to start your career."

She couldn't stay, someone would find out eventually, something would slip out. She began to wish she could tell Lissina. The garden was quiet, ready for secrets, she opened her mouth ready to blurt everything out. Lissina had come to her own decision, she cupped her hand around the back of Mika's neck and kissed her. In shock, Mika didn't return it.

"Think about staying. My father would find a good place for you." The invitation was clear. Lissina smiled and picked a flower from those on Mika's lap. She walked off, twirling it in her fingers and smiling while Mika sat in shock. She was a girl and Lissina thought she was a boy. Tears came into her eyes, Lissina thought she was a good marriage prospect, that was why her father had been so pleasant.

For a wild moment she actually contemplated it. Marriage, the perfect alibi. Then she thought of the marriage night, what would she tell Lissina? She choked back a laugh, "Sorry dear, I've not just got problems getting it up, I haven't got one to start with..." It wouldn't work. Lissina would be furious with her. She could only hope everyone would think she'd panicked at the thought of marriage. Mika carefully put the flowers back on the seat and walked slowly to the classroom. The rest of the day wasn't helped by Lissina smiling at her. Jenna was obviously in on the secret and the rest had twigged by the end of the day. The teasing was horrendous and Mika escaped with relief.

She lay in her bed sniffing the sachet of vineflower she'd made and thought of the musician. Typical Ackbarr looks, swarthy skin, broad face and dark eyes. The way he coaxed his instrument to sing for him. Mika wondered if he had calluses on his fingertips and what they'd feel like. She thought of the differences between his solid body and Jace's leanness and shivered, there was a grace in a different way. She shook her head, she was supposed to be a boy and after Rylan's attentions, she didn't want another relationship. She sighed, either way it didn't look as though she'd get much sleep.

He remained in her mind for days afterwards, remembering his fingers and the way he leant over his gitern. That look in his eyes as he played. The boys assumed she was mooning over Lissina, Lissina preened and clung to her side.

Fed up with herself, she finally went to see Marta. Marta had her own little annex attached to the main house, its own door into the street. Mika hadn't been inside before, Marta was as jealous of her privacy as she was.

Mika knocked nervously, "You said I could talk if I needed to?"

Marta invited her in. The room was tiny and cosy, hangings on the wall, a small shuttered window looking out onto the courtyard. A tiny stove had a kettle waiting nearby. It felt welcoming and warm, like Marta herself.

Mika took a breath steadying herself, "I've got a problem. There's a man I like. He doesn't know I'm a girl." She snorted. "In fact, he doesn't know I exist. I want to get to know him. As a girl."

"Who is he?"

"The gitern player we saw playing the other night."

Marta laughed, "Ezra? He has a reputation." Mika flushed - typical. "Still," She gave Mika a calculating look, "It may give you an advantage if you approach him in the right way. I'll help you get to talk to him as a girl, the rest is up to you." She sat straighter, "You have any money saved from that allowance you get?"

"Yes."

"I will buy the fabric for you and we will make some clothes. Simple jewellery. You will be my cousin from the country. While you are helping me sew, the rest of the house will be told that I am helping you with language skills. One evening a week should do it." Mika opened her mouth to protest, wanting to move quicker. "No. Any more and they won't believe it. Ezra isn't going anywhere or if he does, then you may want to reconsider. Now I think blues and greens will suit you, any favourites?"

They sewed her dresses in the evening together with Marta talking her through the niceties of Ackbarr womanhood. Mika became aware of Marta's enjoyment as she spoke of Ezra's past, his habits of flirtation, his love of the chase and how Mika could use that to her advantage. Mika felt the excitement building in the pit of her stomach. Despite enjoying the freedom of men's clothing, she was surprised to find she looked forward to wearing pretty clothes again, especially when she saw Lissina in yet another new set of dresses.

The evening they finished, Marta took her up to her bedroom to put the clothes on. The long restrictive skirts were strange after striding in boots for so long. She had to remember to contain her movements, be delicate, not use the free swinging gestures and taking up of room that she'd become used to. She remembered the day she'd met Rylan and felt ill.

Marta cocked her head when she saw her. "Not bad. This will need to come in further. You've a long slim body, let's show it off." She pinched the fabric in at the waist, "But the drape is correct and the colour brings out your eyes. Now," She pulled a scarf over Mika's hair. "I will get you a wig this week. No, don't argue, at the moment you look Cassai and although I think he'd love the exotic, you'll be too easy to spot. A soft brown will go with your skin and eyes I think."

Marta and Mika walked out of her private door into the street. They turned away from the larger door of Belindros, despite it being the quickest way to the house where the concert was. Mika felt vulnerable in her skirts. She remembered to keep her strides short and tucked her arm into Marta's to steady herself. Marta was humming softly, a sparkle in her eye. Mika wondered if she'd ever done this for herself and was too shy to ask.

The house came too quickly for Mika, her mouth was dry as they entered and allowed their cloaks to be taken. The merchant was puffed up in his pride of having the musicians performing at his house. Other people milled around and talked. Mika sat, her feet and knees together, she'd not felt this conspicuous for months. By the time the musicians arrived, she was so tense that Marta had taken her hand and started rubbing it gently. He was there. Sitting at the back, a smile on his face, laughing quietly with one of the other musicians. Mika forgot everything as they started and the music swept her away.

Her eyes unfocussed with the music and she relaxed. She casually gazed over the people in front and she jumped as she met Ezra's eyes. She ducked her head, stomach tight again. Marta's hand was a little warm now, the whole room was warm, she didn't care. She glanced again, he was still looking. She allowed herself to drift, feeling her cheeks grow hot. Several times during the evening their eyes met, a jolt going through her and each time she looked away first.

At the end, Marta whispered for them to go. Mika nearly protested, the merchant had food and good wine. Marta shook her head, "We need to leave now, people at home will miss us otherwise."

They escaped into the night air. Marta chuckled as they walked, "I believe I'm enjoying this almost as much as you are."

"I'm not sure if I enjoyed it." She flushed again, remembering his stare.

"He certainly noticed you. Now we need to keep him noticing."

They went to several concerts, Mika had a list in her room and Marta made the decisions. Not this one – too close to the last performance, we'll do this one instead. Ezra watched from the back as he played, growing larger in her vision until it felt as though he leaned towards her, playing only for the two of them. She didn't need to act her shyness as he began to smile when he saw her in the audience. The mischief in his eye as he caught hers and the cant of his head as he played filled her dreams, pushing aside those of the jungle.

He finally caught them about to leave one evening. "I don't believe we've been introduced?" His question was directed at Marta, Mika was the one he gazed at. He was only a few years older than her, five at the most she'd heard. Born into a lower ranking family, his talent had caught the attention of a childless noble. He'd had everything bestowed on him since and it showed. His confidence bordered on arrogance, suddenly she felt like slapping him for the assumption that she wanted his attentions.

Marta caught Mika's look and smiled, "No, I don't believe we have." Mika's gaze was icy as Marta introduced them.

His manners immediately became perfect, "May I offer you a drink?"

"Thank you, we were just leaving," Mika snapped. His reply was interrupted by the host attempting to introduce him to other nobles. Mika turned with the pretence of not seeing his look of frustration. Marta gave him an indulgent smile as they left.

She laughed as they walked into the alley. "Well done Mika. Was that real or feigned?"

"I just couldn't believe it, he's so full of himself." Mika was sputtering, she wasn't sure why he'd upset her so much.

"Well, you've got his attention which is what you wanted. He'll come back to find out more next time, you watch."

Mika snorted.

Chapter 17

Mika sneaked out of the city gates several times a week now. She'd become more friendly with the guardsmen over time, bringing treats and chatting to them about their various wives and mistresses. She learnt their rotas, finding out which guards were pickier about letting people in or out.

She had no idea of what happened while she was changed, she only knew she was dangerous. If Belindros was correct then she should be a cat and the prints seemed to indicate it. She'd bought a bone with her this time, wondering if it would help distract her conscious mind. She stripped and lay close, smelling it and following the tickling sensation over her skin. It was a subconscious thing. Mika had learnt how the sensation changed and stopped if she paid too much attention. The bone was nearly touching her face, the iron smell of blood filled her nostrils. Without being fully aware, she flicked her tongue out and tasted. She bared her teeth, waited for the stretch, the rippling into unconsciousness as she stopped being Mika and became something else.

Slowly as the weeks passed the change became more fluid. Sometimes it was stronger, especially after she'd seen Jace. At these times she made the decision to fight the urge, realising she had to control it. She started to make a note of them in her head and realised that after a stressful day, the dreams were stronger. She took care of herself, not allowing herself to be upset by anything and she began to get a reputation for calmness, both in the classroom and at the hospital. With a shock she remembered how her mother had always been calm and found herself wondering how her mother would have dealt with changing like Mika did.

Mika practised at her control, unaware it was having other effects on her. Small signs from the patients she attended, the sheen of sweat, dilation of eyes and muscle tics became obvious, helping with diagnosis. She became smoother in her fighting with Gavin and her instructors, noticing the little changes in how they flexed and shifted, anticipating moves before they happened. Her reactions became effortless as every muscle in her body reached optimal performance. Other people on seeing her fight, remarked quietly that she was moving more like the King's Advisor these days and they wondered what the outcome would be if they ever met in combat. They speculated if it might be a Cassai trait but none dared mention it within Jace's hearing.

Ezra's image continued to flick into Mika's brain at inconvenient moments. She'd swear to herself, disliking the hold he had over her. For an entire week she refused to think about going to any more concerts despite Marta's encouragement. When Mika gave in and went, Ezra's eyes fastened onto Mika immediately, barely leaving her.

During the interval, Marta left to get drinks. Mika was pondering the sweet nibbles on the table when a voice said, "These ones are remarkably nice."

She looked up to find Ezra standing next to her and holding out a plate of tiny pastries that happened to be her favourites. Mika shook her head, suddenly not hungry. She had no way of removing herself, a group stood behind them and he'd effectively pinned her into the space next to the table.

His instrument was slung over his back and his eyes were warm as they tried to peer into hers. Teasing the girls in her class was easy, this was different, abruptly she didn't need to act coy. She'd been too young to do much flirting with her brother's friends. A sweetly stolen kiss, the occasional admiring comment had been all she'd had and chaperoned by her brother's scornful tongue, his friends hadn't taken advantage. With Alma, she'd giggled over various lads of their own age. There'd been no courtship with Rylan. She now had an interested man in front of her and she didn't know what to do with him.

Sensing her confusion he asked "Did you enjoy the performance?"

"Yes."

"At least you seem to be listening, unlike most." His voice was pitched for their ears only. She looked up, startled. He shrugged with a disgusted look on his face, "Most are simply here to be seen. I could be playing 'Johnny jingles his dangles' in the nude for all they'd notice." She smothered a giggle, as Mikon she knew all ten verses and sang them frequently, much to the delight of Jon.

He smiled back, his eyes catching hers again. A warmth flared between them and she flushed. A disturbance to the side, Marta had arrived with the drinks and Ezra retreated into his polite self, enquiring after Marta's health and enjoyment. Mika sat and listened to the second performance, oblivious to the world as Ezra played to her in the audience.

Through the weeks Ezra became more insistent, wanting to know where she lived and what her father did. She blocked his questions, frustrated that she had no easy answers. Marta conveniently disappeared for them to talk each time, but she still despaired over how to take it further, she couldn't keep lying. People were beginning to notice his interest, watching her out of the corner of their eyes through the performance, wanting to listen in to their conversation and asking her questions afterwards. One evening he pushed a piece of paper into her hand while greeting her. She tucked it into her sleeve pocket for later.

She read it in her room, she hadn't been brave enough to tell Marta. He wanted to meet in the park, he was free and would wait over the next few nights. She knew she'd be safe. She'd seen couples strolling there in the summer and autumn, chaperoned by the sheer number of people.

Mika thought all day, changing her mind a dozen times and then gave up. She liked him. He was arrogant about his playing, but he had a right to be and his looks, well, he was no more arrogant about them than her brother. The number of times she'd caught her brother checking himself in the mirror before talking to this girl or that. She sniggered at the memories of foiling his advances. The bucket of cold water had worked beautifully, carefully aimed to only soak him, not the girl. He'd been furious with her for days after that one. She sighed, wondering what his reaction would be to Ezra, then shook her head and went to find Marta to ask about using her rooms.

"You will have to tell him who you are at some point," Marta warned.

"Yes, but not tonight. Will you help?"

Jon was delighted to help, subterfuge was something he loved. They disappeared out together through the main gate, Mika knocking on Marta's outside door five minutes later. Jon, dressed in old clothes kept an eye out as she walked quickly away in her dresses.

At the park she walked alone for a while and several young men stopped to ask if she had a partner for the evening. She shook her head each time, stomach tight with nerves, unused to the attention as a woman. Eventually she took the plunge and walked to the area where Ezra had said he would meet her. She saw him first, his eyes narrowed and unguarded for once as he watched the people walk by. He spotted her a moment later and a huge smile lit his face. He took her hand, tucking it into his elbow like the rest of the couples.

They spent the evening talking, Ezra kept the conversation light, sharing the pastries he bought. He offered to walk her home, laughing ruefully when she refused - she couldn't let him find out where she lived. He kissed her fingers and asked to see her again the next evening. Mika shook her head, not wanting to say that she had fighting practice with Gavin and they agreed on the evening after.

Jon joined her on the way back, saying Ezra had made no attempt to follow, just watched her walk away. Jon made the appropriate mooning faces, rolling his eyes and simpering until she pushed him away and told him to check the door to Marta's house.

Mika stopped going to the performances and Marta agreed with reluctance. People had been noticing Ezra staring, she couldn't risk the curiosity, although she missed his playing. She started to hint to him that she wasn't what she seemed and he followed her trail of thought with fascination. He seemed content to seduce her with his eyes, did nothing else that was outside the bounds of propriety in public and yet that made her flush, much to his enjoyment. She sensed he was enjoying the chase as much as she was enjoying being chased. A restless urge began, with her starting to tease him as much as he did her.

One evening they were sitting on a low wall, in sight of people but away from them. "You know I am not from Ackbarr."

"Yes, you've said." His eyes looked mischievous. "A lady of mystery, I like it."

She took a deep breath and said, "I'm wearing a wig."

He pretended shock. "Are you going to show me what you look like without it? Am I going to hate your real hair? Don't tell me you don't have any hair underneath it." His barrage of questions were accompanied by a grin, he didn't care and she knew it.

"The reason why I've not let you walk me back home is because I'm pretending to be a boy there. They don't know I'm a girl."

That did silence him. He stared at the people walking by and eventually asked, "Why?"

"My prospects weren't good as a girl. I've no male relations to look after me. I was taken on by my current master as a boy and I've not had the chance to do anything about it." She added defensively, "Besides, I like learning, I can't do that as a girl." She watched him anxiously, trying to work out his reaction.

"I take it Marta isn't your aunt?"

"No."

He seemed calm. "I've seen feisty noble girls doing pretty much what they want. Why shouldn't you?"

"You don't mind?" She abruptly realised she was putting herself into his hands, he could choose to tell the authorities. What would she do to keep in his good books, how far would she go to stop him? If enough people knew, even Belindros wouldn't be able to protect her.

He grinned and suppressed the movement that said he wanted to sweep her into his arms, "Do I mind? Great gods, you've got more balls than half the nobility!" His eyes flashed with pride. Mika couldn't believe it, her brother would approve of this man and so would her father. She ducked her head, hiding the tears. He mistook the reason and tucked a finger under her chin, lifting it. "You don't need to worry about me telling anyone. If anyone finds out, then I'll take you away. We'll deal with it together." She blinked as he raised her fingers to his lips, the only gesture he was allowed in public. "Come to my place tomorrow? I'd love to see you without the wig. Come in your boy clothes if it's easier. Which master are you apprenticed to?"

"Belindros."

"The Medici?" His face was impressed, "He's supposed to be a hard taskmaster, I've met him several times." She shrugged and he laughed, "Now I can believe you are pretending to be a boy." Other couples began to drift closer and he stood, proudly tucking her hand into his elbow.

She tugged at his shoulder, "I can't come tomorrow."

"Why?"

She looked embarrassed, "I have lessons tomorrow night."

"He keeps you working during the evening? What sort of lessons?"

"Um, combat." She felt herself flushing as he regarded her with disbelief.

"What sort of combat?"

"Fencing mostly."

He shook his head, "I'm going to have to get used to this. The night after then?" He bent towards her with a grin and whispered, "I'll have pastries." He knew her weakness for the crisp pastries full of nuts and honey and she nodded laughing.

The night after, she slid out the courtyard gates with Jon to guide her. Ezra had given her his address, it was a place closer to the walls of the city and was rundown, but clean. Washing hung out on the dark stone balconies. Everything was stone in Ackbarr. Mika was suddenly homesick for the green leafy depths of Cassai, the clean smells of the trees and the rough whitewashed walls of her parent's home. She shook herself as Jon skipped away, she knew he was looking forward to an evening with old friends. She didn't want to know what else he'd get up to.

Ezra peered down from a second storey balcony and yelled his delight at seeing her. She was greeted as a mate, slapped on the back and pulled upstairs. He slammed the door shut and stood inches away, inspecting her. "You look like a boy."

She huffed at him, "What did you expect?"

"Is that your real hair?"

"Not entirely, mine's darker." He touched it gently, brushing his fingers through and noticed her flinch.

"What is it?"

"Nothing." Despite her best efforts, images of Rylan had risen. A man's hands on her, owning her and hurting. Her throat swelled tight.

"What's the matter?"

Tears filled her eyes, she turned away, "I'm sorry."

"No. I want to know. Tell me. Whatever it is." He had hold of her arms and was trying to get her to look at him. She could tell he was trying to keep his hands gentle and the terror still rose. He was stronger, he could hurt without trying.

"Please don't."

"Tell me." His voice was a whisper.

His gentle insistence slowly won through and she stumbled through the marriage, not wanting to give too much detail. Trying not to cry, the dam was holding the tears back, but only just. She said she'd run away, not wanting to explain about waking to find Rylan dead in their bed. Her voice was dry as his hands rubbed her arms and he listened. She stopped, unable to speak further.

"Bastard." His voice was matter of fact.

She looked up, startled. "He was young, he didn't know."

"No excuse for not thinking. You're smaller than him, it stands to reason you're more delicate. I was never like that." His fingers brushed her hair again. "It's not like that. Some people never discover it."

He gently pulled her into his arms and held her. She stayed there, stiff, breathing into his shoulder and something broke. Her knees gave way as she cried for herself, her lost baby, the strange changing she'd had to deal with and every lack she'd had over the past months. He picked her up awkwardly and sat on the bed, still cradling her and allowed her to cry herself out. Eventually she stopped and peered at him.

"Better now?"

Sniffing, she nearly punched him, he had a smug look on his face. She stood to get away from his disturbing closeness. "I must look a mess."

"Yep." He sprawled back onto his bed, feet mussing the covers. "Still look gorgeous though, I prefer you without the wig. Are you Cassai stock?"

Mika nodded and looked around his room to distract herself. His clothes were slung on the chairs, caught up in the chest lid and there was food on the table, plates waiting to be washed. Music was scattered in piles on the table, falling onto the floor, replacement strings uncoiling and his music case tucked carefully on a shelf. She wiped her face on her sleeve, "This place is a mess."

"Must be a woman." He laughed as she flung a shirt at him, "Hey, that one's clean..." he sniffed it and pulled a face, "...ish."

Any free evenings became precious to Mika as they began to meet more regularly. She made excuses for going out so she could spend her time with Ezra. Being part of the royal household, he also had performances and other demands on his time at the whim of the nobility. Jon complained in private that she was mooning after him. He'd met Ezra and approved in his strangely adult way. Mika was pleased, she had so few friends who knew her real sex, it was important they got on.

There were times when she came dressed as a woman and others in her boy's clothes. Ezra was delighted by the contrast in her behaviour. She was simply amazed no one clicked that she was one and the same discovering that people looked at clothes, not what was underneath.

She took Ezra to the menagerie - she'd found that her apprentice robes were enough to get them in. They passed Jace several times and she made a point of larking about, being more of a boy in his presence. Ezra caught on immediately, though asked her why afterwards. Mika shook her head, unable to explain her antipathy to Jace.

Mika leaned against the fence separating them from the cats and stared with the rest of the crowd. The cats turned to watch her, their eyes slitted. She tried to reach out with her mind and felt as though she was grasping empty air. She wondered how Jace managed. Her own command of herself was becoming more consistent these days. She spent the times when Ezra was performing, practising her own changing, twisting herself through and back. Attempting to remember her time while changed and trying to stop the change halfway through was difficult. The cat within her resisted but remembering Jace she kept on trying.

She'd been staring too long. Ezra nudged her, he wanted to know why the cats fascinated her so much. She explained how they were loved by her people and the legends of a cat intermingling with the royal family. She shivered as she spoke of it, could it be true? He shook his head, not seeing her fascination and dragged her back to his rooms for some more interesting explorations of his own.

"I've decided." Ezra was in his favourite place later on, sprawled across his bed and plucking idly at the strings on his instrument, "I'm going to seduce you."

His eyes lazily wandered over her as she slung her cloak on against the rain outside.

"What was it you've been doing so far?" She flushed, she still wasn't used to a man looking at her in this way.

He grinned, "That's just a warm up." He swung himself onto his feet and kissed her soundly, "I intend to have you begging." Mika froze in his arms, torn between anxiety and delight. "But not just yet. I can wait, that's half the fun." She did punch him then and he folded up, laughing.

Chapter 18

Lissina's campaign to capture the boy she thought Mika was, wasn't helped by her father asking Mika to accompany his daughter to the palace on certain afternoons to meet her cousins. He couldn't make his approval plainer. Mika struggled to walk the fine line between enjoying Lissina's company and following the signals that she was giving out. She wondered if she'd been that obvious to Ezra and decided she hadn't. In the privacy of his rooms, Ezra had become bolder, pulling her closer, kissing her. Mika flushed thinking about him. She'd began to trust him, to respond more to his explorations.

Lissina's voice caught her attention, she'd been talking and Mika hadn't been listening. Lissina huffed, "I don't know why I bother…" She stopped as Jace walked by, the cat bumping against his legs, muscles rippling under its velvety skin. They both moved in the same way, a wild stride that didn't belong in the surroundings, challenging the civilisation around them.

Rebuffed by Mika, Lissina smiled brilliantly at Jace and his attention was caught by her. His mouth opened briefly, Mika thought it was the beginning of a smile, then she caught the sharp movement of his chest. It was like a cat smelling. She'd seen the little cats do that at home, they'd sniff her mother's fingers open mouthed and then purr as she scratched their ears. His mouth clicked shut and he bent his head to Lissina in greeting, ignoring Mika.

Mika hurried Lissina up to her cousin's rooms at the palace and said her goodbyes, troubled by Jace's nearness.

"When is your birthday Jon?" Ezra asked. They were walking around the park, the dry cold air whipping around. Jon had joined them for once.

Mika blinked in confusion - birthday? Jon shrugged, kicking against the stone wall, "Dunno."

"Didn't you ever have one?" Jon just looked uncomfortable. "What about yours?" he asked Mika.

"My what?"

"Birthday." Seeing her look of confusion, he explained, "You know, to celebrate the day you were born?"

"We don't do that in Cassai. We celebrate at Midsummer. It's a big festival, everyone becomes a year older at once."

"So, did you celebrate this summer?"

"No, I was too busy." She looked at the ground, her parents would have been upset and missing both her and Kaylan. Two children gone.

Ezra rolled his eyes and then looked thoughtful. "Never mind Jon, you could use the Cassai method too, have it at midsummer."

"But that means I have to wait nearly a year!" Mika and Ezra laughed at Jon's indignation.

She had begun to wake from the changes with vague dreams of stalking through the countryside. She encouraged them, believing it was the only way she could remember what she'd done. The colours were different from her sleeping dreams. They were monochrome, with the smells and movement sharper.

She walked through the countryside on her afternoons off, with the eerie feeling of having been to places before. Jon got thoroughly spooked when she pushed through what appeared to be impenetrable bushes to find a tiny stream and was unable to say how she'd known about it.

Mika panicked the night she woke to find a carcass next to her. She'd become used to changing out in the country, with only a few deep breaths and tickling the right place in her brain to trigger the change. She came into consciousness curled around a sack of broken bones, the blood stained fleece accusing her of a theft she couldn't remember. Her stomach felt heavy and she fought to stop herself vomiting at the thought of eating raw flesh.

She dragged the remains into a copse and hid it in the bushes, hoping it wouldn't be found. She listened hard to the conversations of her classmates the next day, worrying that the dead sheep had been discovered. No mention was made.

Several nights later it happened again. A dismembered sheep gazing into her eyes as she opened her own. This time she heard people in the distance. Naked and covered with blood, she ran, bent double to the nearest cover. As a predator she had no fear of humans, they'd be further down the food chain. As a girl, she had no doubt that the attentions of any man who found her naked would be very unwelcome and she wasn't sure if she could change at will purely to kill a man for making assumptions.

Shaking with cold and the fear of being caught she dressed, thankful her clothes weren't too far away. She sluiced herself down in a stream and sneaked back through the city. It took her a long time to stop shaking in bed and ages to warm up. This time she did hear rumours from the boys in her class. A large animal had been preying on a local farmer's sheep, they'd seen a shadow leaving the corpse. Patrols would be sent out and the livestock kept in.

Mika stayed inside for several weeks after that, setting herself the challenge of changing one part of herself instead. Staying conscious while watching her hand widen and fingertips shrink nearly made her vomit. She persisted, certain she'd need the discipline. Mika touched the thick claws and the soft fur as if they belonged to something else, not quite believing the cat's paw on the end of her slender wrist. She could feel a cold numbness running down the length of her arm and remembered Jon asking if it hurt to change and not being able to answer. Her muscles spasmed uncontrollably, making her arm shake. She couldn't feel anything past her shoulder. Halting the change and keeping it stable wasn't easy, sweat poured from her as she forced her body to do what she wanted.

When the rumours had died down, on Jon's suggestion she started to set herself challenges to distract herself from thieving. She hid a bone a mile away from her changing spot, tried to keep it in her mind as she changed. When she woke, it was there beside her, cracked and broken. She shuddered at the teeth marks and then swore as she realised she'd have to walk naked back to where she'd left her clothes. She took more care after that, hiding a tunic close by as well. She set herself harder challenges, got Jon to hide things for her other self, following the scent from an old tunic to find the treasure.

Lissina came into class looking pleased with herself, tilting her head to show off a new set of earrings. She and Jenna whispered through the break and Jenna looking worried.

"Mikon," Lissina hissed at her before the tutor walked in, "I did it."

"Did what?"

"He let me, I stroked the cat." She was full of herself.

"What?"

"Jace. I asked him when I saw him in the palace yesterday evening." She giggled. "I was terrified and he smells of that stuff he smokes. Then he smiled at me." She sighed and leaned over further, "He's so handsome when he smiles. He got the cat to lie down, put his hand on its head and told me to stroke it. It didn't want to let me at first, it growled. I nearly wet myself, but he took my hand and made me touch it. Its fur is so soft, so thick, I nearly lost my fingers in it." She stopped talking, lost in memories.

"Lissina, he frightens you because he's dangerous."

She tossed her head, "He can be really charming when he wants to be. I think you're jealous."

The tutor walked in and that was the end to the conversation. Mika thought of Lissina trying to touch her when she'd changed and shuddered. No way would she allow that in her other form. Only Jace's control kept the cat from running on a rampage. Her mind raced desperately to think of a way to discourage Lissina and failed through the tiredness of disturbed nights.

She met up with Ezra that night, away from his playing to the court.

"You are really bad for my practising. I should be looking at this," He waved his hand at the sheaf of music discarded on the floor, "And here I am attempting to get your clothes off." He pulled her close and started undoing her shirt ties while kissing her neck.

"What am I going to do about Lissina?"

"Hmm?"

She pushed at him, "Lissina, I'm worried about her and Jace." Ezra muttered a swear word into her neck as he slid his hand up her shirt and discovered her corset. "Seduce her then. Give her what she wants. Gods woman, you're tied up tighter than an usurer's arse."

"I can't seduce her. It'd be easy if I was a boy."

Sighing at not being able to get to bare skin, he propped himself on his elbow with a lazy smile. "I could get you some lessons at Drutha's. Then, by the time you'd finished with her, she wouldn't care what you were." He wagged a finger, "Conditions being, that I get to watch all the lessons." Mika rolled her eyes and sat up to peel off her shirt.

Later that week Mika lay in her own bed and worried for Lissina, she'd refused to listen, charmed by the attentions of a handsome older man. She was still happy enough to spend time with Mika, but the conversation always came back to Jace and pointing out his similarities to Mika.

She squirmed, wondering if he did actually like Lissina. It was perfectly possible. Lissina was pretty, Mika had to admit, with delicate features, vivacious eyes and the mass of dark curly hair. Unlike his reputation suggested, Jace was always impeccably behaved around her. Mika sourly decided he did it to wind her up. Every time he went past, Lissina would sigh and Mika would get bombarded with questions.

Mika muttered to herself, was she any better? She lay and thought of the previous night, Ezra had outdone himself. She'd slipped into his rooms later than normal, wanting to surprise him after a concert and found he'd not gone out after all.

She'd stopped delighted by the scene, wine and food had awaited her. The usual lamps he had lit for reading music in the evenings had been blown out on her arrival, the smell still lingering. The candle lit room made for a cosy space in the dark, the mess of clothes had been shoved into a corner and the sheaves of music and clutter faded into the dimness. He leant against the door frame, inviting her in with a mischievous gleam in his eye.

He'd teased her over her sudden shyness and she was aware of a tension throughout the meal. A nervous expectation, threaded through with the memories of her wedding with Rylan. She drank little and noticed Ezra didn't touch much either. He refused to rush, insisting they enjoy the food he'd bought.

Ezra had been extremely decided in his attentions, allowing her to set the pace, but refusing her any chance to get away. She'd tightly held onto her fears, not wanting to think about her earlier experiences and allowed him to win her over with soft kisses and gentle caresses. His insistence she explore him as much as he did her, calmed her fears, allowing her to concentrate on the feeling of his flesh against hers.

She'd lain in the dark afterwards, stroking Ezra's warm side while he dozed in her arms. In the end, his teasing that he'd have her begging hadn't been far off, he'd simply not factored in his own reactions to the gentle wind up he'd performed. She marvelled at the softness of his skin, she'd never touched Rylan like this. Ezra grunted and shifted away as she found a ticklish spot, then pulled her close. She giggled and persisted in exploring until he caught her fingers, kissed them and put them elsewhere. Mika thought further, Rylan had never touched her like this.

Sensing her change of mood, he tilted her chin, "This bed's too small."

Confused, she asked, "What do you mean?"

"There's only space for two of us in here, not three. Stop thinking about him." Mika opened her mouth. Ezra stopped her reply by kissing her and saying, "I can tell, you go all stiff. Now stop it." He tucked her back into his arms and they dozed, limbs tangled.

Ezra had unpeeled himself reluctantly to light a lamp as she reminded him that she had to go back, otherwise people would ask questions. He insisted on walking her home through the deserted streets despite her being dressed as a boy. He pointed out, with all seriousness, that youths were set upon by strangers in the city. She didn't like to mention she'd been walking the streets on her own in the dead of night for weeks now.

"You're going to lose your reputation by walking boys' home," she teased.

"What reputation?"

She grinned, "Flirt."

"Lover." He qualified with a smile, "And?"

"And what?"

"Do I deserve it?"

She'd ducked her head and smiled, refusing to answer, he didn't need that sort of praise. He'd pulled her into his arms, kissed her and refused to let her go.

Mika had been unable to get away. Ezra, not caring that she looked like a boy in the dark night, kissed her until she gave up and agreed, that yes, he did.

Mika flushed with the memories, she'd had a hard time this morning not to walk down to the kitchen singing. Gavin had grinned and asked who the lucky girl was. Marta had given her a searching look and promptly deflected any extra attention away from her. Jon had been dreadful, all the way up to the palace, teasing her constantly about the moonstruck look on her face.

Chapter 19

Mika saw Jace talking to Lissina in the hall. He leaned over her, his cool features transformed with a brilliant smile. The sight reminded Mika of a predator stalking its prey and Lissina looked transfixed by the older man's charm. Mika noticed Lissina's father talking with another noble close by, torn between concern for his young daughter and pride that she'd caught the attention of someone in the King's favour. Jace caught Mika's eye and whispered something further, something sly that made Lissina giggle, then he kissed her hand and walked away with a smirk for his younger countryman.

"What are you doing?"

"He likes me." Lissina gave a shrug. Mika couldn't help noticing that her pupils were huge and she could smell Sweetroot around her. She tried not to breathe too deeply.

"He gave me these." Lissina showed off her earrings, touching them gently.

"He's dangerous."

Lissina snorted, "I think you're jealous."

"Is that what he said? Lissi, I'm worried for you. I thought we were friends."

"Father's over there." She waved a hand, "I suppose I'd better go to him, don't want to be seen talking to strange men." She giggled again and Mika sighed, there was no way as a boy she could talk to her. She couldn't say why Jace was dangerous. Mika wondered if she should tell Lissina that she was a girl, would it make her listen? She shook her head, if she did there was no guarantee Lissina would keep her secret.

Everyone was on a high, the midwinter festival would come shortly. The weather was dry and cold. A thin layer of frost spread over the buildings and cobbles in the mornings, the exposed parts burning off as the sun rose, deepening into an iron hardness in sheltered corners.

Jon raced around, twice as excited as everyone else. Whilst Jon's studies were going well, getting his attention became harder as the weeks went by. Mika saw the other apprentices having the same problems with their boys. Jon hadn't experienced the midwinter festival in a proper home before, only seen the decorations outside, the bonfires and masked frivolities. Each addition to the house sent him into further spasms of delight. Mika had her own surprises for him, hidden from his quick eyes and knew Gavin and the others had similar ideas.

It became a relief to escape to the cool quiet corridors of the hospice. The usual coughs and slips on icy cobbles affected the population and Mika was kept busy. Her knowledge had increased to the point where she no longer had to follow Enos around and she was expected to deal with her own patients. The first week of practice was terrifying, until she realised they were giving her the easier patients to deal with. Abran or another Medici would check on her work, quietly suggesting improvements. As Enos had said, the patients ignored her heritage, she was simply Medici.

Belindros had caught cold after cold this winter. Mika watched with concern while everyone fussed around him. For once he didn't appear to enjoy the attention, his usually acerbic comments muted and his voice hoarse. Mika would read various books to him, while he coughed and dribbled in a pile of misery. Marta coaxed him into eating. Jon sat in his room to study, attempting to read aloud and being snapped at whenever he got something wrong.

The week before the festival, Lissina caught Mika at the end of the lessons. "Will you walk me through the festival next week? Father says he would be happy for you to do so." She played with her hair, twining it around her fingers, sure of Mika's reply. The others stopped in the doorway, waiting.

Mika was flustered, she'd promised to meet Ezra. Their relationship had got to the point where she was having problems concentrating during the day if she wasn't careful. She'd discovered a mischievous side to herself that had her constantly thinking up new ideas to tease him with. Every spare moment they had together she cherished. Ezra was in demand constantly by the nobility at the moment and he grumbled over the lack of time they had together.

"I can't."

Lissina's eyes flashed, "Fine, I'll find someone else then." She flounced off, pulling Jenna with her. Jenna shrugged at Mika and followed, to the unhelpful cat-calls of the other boys. Mika shrugged off their invites for the park as she left.

The night of the festival, tiny lights were tucked into crevices of the buildings, giving the look of the starlit sky coming down to rest in the city. From above the walls, the real stars glittered sharp and cold. Mika had never seen anything like it. Couples walked around the markets in masks, small children dashing about underfoot. Ezra dressed up and Mika came out in her skirts to meet him. They laughed together, him buying spiced wine that went to her head nearly as much as the warm kisses he gave her in the cold air.

She slipped in through Marta's door, shutting it quietly. Her head was still a little muzzy from the wine she'd drunk. The room was warm after the chill outside and she could hear a bustle beyond in the main house. Still unsure as to what ceremonies went on at this time of year, she dressed quickly back into her boy's clothes.

The lamps were on full as she went into the hall. A number of guards stood around she didn't recognise, the servants moving amongst them. Despite the decorations it didn't seem festive here. People looked worried, talking quietly.

Marta caught her, "Go to the private examination room, knock first. Lin wants you now."

Confused, she ran down the corridor. The door opened and she found a couple sitting and waiting with tense faces. She recognised Lissina's father, his solemnity now stone-faced. Her mother she'd rarely seen although she could see the resemblance in her size and the delicate hands and feet, with the same soft curly dark hair.

"Lissina?"

Belindros came through the curtained alcove, "In here."

She walked in, her heart in her throat without knowing why. Lissina lay on the couch. Blood was everywhere, there were scrapes on her face and hands and she huddled into herself, clutching the blanket covering her. Her eyes looked dazed until they focused on Mika and she moaned, turning away, trying to hide in the back of the couch.

Belindros turned Mika around and took her back into the corridor. "Do you know anything about this?"

Speechless, she shook her head, "I've been with a friend, I've only just got back." His face was stony.

"Marta can vouch for me, she knows everything." Her heart sank further, she was going to have to tell him she was a girl. "What happened?"

"She won't say. I have my suspicions." He continued, "Have you been anywhere near the park tonight?" She shook her head, Ezra had walked them around the main lit areas then dragged her back to his rooms for a celebration of their own.

"She was found wandering around there. Her father brought her here a short while ago." He watched her carefully. "She has been violated in a way that could implicate only one person. I need to know where you've been before I make the accusation." Mika opened her mouth to reply when a shout from the room interrupted them. Belindros turned to go back in and she was left feeling helpless.

She slowly walked back to her rooms. Jon had disturbed at her step outside his room, only to be snapped at to go back to sleep. He did so with the natural ability of a street child or small animal, if the trouble didn't concern him then it could wait. Mika sat with her head in her hands. Jace had raped Lissina and he'd done it while she'd been with Ezra. Why hadn't she gone with Lissina? She could have met with Ezra later, he would have waited. Deep down she knew it was because she'd got impatient with Lissina's childish crush on her. This was her fault.

Unable to stand being on her own, she went down to the kitchen. She sat in the quiet bustle, nursing a hot drink and stared into the fire. Eventually Belindros called her into his study, he looked old as he sat behind his desk.

"Well?"

"She fancied me. When I didn't show her all the interest she wanted, she decided to go after someone like me. I tried to warn her off, she thought I was jealous." Her voice was flat.

He nodded grimly, "And you are full-blooded Cassai."

"Yes."

"One of the royal family?"

"Yes."

"I guessed as much. Can you change?"

"Yes." She barely breathed it.

"Jace knows?"

"I think he's guessed."

Belindros shifted impatiently, "Why do you think I've been trying to keep you away from him boy? Why I didn't mind you bleaching your hair to look like a full blood. What I can't understand is why he went after her. He normally goes for blonde or as blonde as he can get around here." He rubbed his tired eyes. "Just to make sure we get this right, who are your parents?"

"My father is Koren, the Cassai ambassador. My mother is Ayanna, she's the member of the royal family."

His fingers became still and he snapped back, "I know who she is Kaylan." He nodded as she gaped at the use of her brother's name. "I guessed who you might be when I found you wandering in Fenin. Your father met me after you went missing, asked me to keep an eye out for you. He was desperate. He couldn't spend any more time looking and people were starting to ask questions. I've spent all this fucking time trying to keep you out of trouble and you go looking for it."

Mika gulped, "I'm not Kaylan." It was the hardest thing she'd ever said, "I'm his sister, Mika."

The blood drained out of his face. Every wrinkle showed and for the first time he actually looked his age. "My god." He dropped his face into his hands, there was a long silence between them. Mika sat waiting, there wasn't anything else to say.

He shifted to prop his head up on his elbow, all vitality drained out of him, "That poor girl, when you met him for the first time, she was with you."

"Yes."

"And you met him at other points when she was around."

"Yes." She could hardly breathe.

"How often?"

"Over several months." She tried to think through the tiredness, "It must have been every few weeks, maybe more often, I can't remember exactly."

"She was with you every time?"

"Most times. We were in the same class. Her father liked me to escort her to the palace to see her cousins."

"He smelt you. He assumed it was her." They locked eyes. Mika went cold, remembering the looks of confusion.

"He thought I was a boy."

"It's the only thing that saved you. He thought you were a rival. No, not a rival. He knew he could beat you at any point. He was playing with you, trying to get you to react. This was deliberate, he wants you to try something." His face firmed, "We have to get you out of here."

"No. My studies. Jon..."

"Jon can go with you. I'll find somewhere, use an excuse. If we are lucky, he will think you've run from him."

"No."

"Don't you understand?" His fist thumped the desk, "You've got no cover now. If he finds out you're a girl..." He trailed off and re-started, "The King has always wanted an army of killers. That's why he tolerates Jace, no other reason. If either of them finds out that you are a girl, then you are dead or as good as."

Mika hadn't thought she could become colder, she began to shake. Rape. What she'd had with Rylan would be nothing compared with Jace. She remembered the tugging between them. He'd want to control her. A sickness spread through her stomach. She nodded.

"Tonight. Get your things together. If we are lucky then Jace will think you've run. We can't risk him realising what you are. Wake Gavin and send him to me."

Chapter 20

Gavin seemed to be able to go from sleeping to full alertness in a second. He strode over to Belindros' study, still pulling on his shirt. At any other point Mika would have been attempting not to watch the muscles moving under the smooth skin. This evening she couldn't care, Gavin could have been parading around naked and she wouldn't have noticed. She woke Jon, told him to pack and sat on her bed, trying to work out what she needed.

Marta came up, found her staring at the wall and helped her pack. Her quiet murmurs helped to reassure Mika. The shock hadn't set in fully yet, everything felt unreal as Marta quizzed her on what she'd need, folded clothes and tucked other items into a set of saddlebags.

"Lissina is sleeping," Marta said. "It's the best healer at the moment." She shook her head, "All Lin can do is to keep washing her out and hope nothing goes septic inside. He hates to feel helpless like this." Mika winced.

They went downstairs, collecting Jon on the way and found Belindros outside waiting for them. Gavin had prepared the horses and a pony for Jon who was yawning.

Belindros hugged her unexpectedly, holding her for a long time. He cupped her face in his hands and said gruffly, "Best damned apprentice I've had and what do I find? He's a girl. I knew you were too good to be true." She wobbled a smile in return. "I've told Gavin. He knows where to take you, there aren't many places where Jace can't go. I'll get you out of the gates."

They led the horses down. Belindros perched on a horse led by Gavin, wrapped up against the cold. The festive decorations were limp in Mika's eyes and her breath caught as she realised she'd not said goodbye to Ezra. She didn't have the time to explain, he'd want to come as well and he couldn't. He was too well known, they'd find her through him. Tears slid quietly down her face, remembering their warm sleepy argument this evening as she'd insisted she leave their bed to go home. How he'd grumbled at her sliding out of his arms and got dressed to walk her through the iron frost. The way he'd kissed her, open mouthed and leant against the wall to watch her go inside. He'd find Marta, would ask where she'd gone. Fear grew as she wondered what he'd do when he found out.

They reached the gates. Belindros slid down with Gavin's help and spoke quietly with the guards. A few murmured words and the gates opened, they mounted on the other side. A note of finality sounded to her as the gates shut behind them, the docks spreading out below. It was no longer a place of sanctuary, a wish she'd had when she'd first arrived.

They trotted their horses, warming them up. The moons were bright, not yet set behind the mountains. A lightness on the horizon showed where morning would come. Mika thought of Lissina lying on the bed. Pale and still, the whimper when she'd seen Mika still made her heart turn over. The frost lay white over everything, steam poured from the nostrils of the horses. A crisp cold night, turning into morning, sparklingly beautiful. A sense of injustice, it shouldn't be like this, not today. She was sharply reminded of the day she'd been told about her brother. The world kept turning whatever happened, without caring.

As the sun rose, Gavin urged them into a canter. Jon clung on grimly, he'd never learnt to ride and had only sat on the pony in the yard. Mika felt her muscles stretch with the unaccustomed exercise. She'd ache tomorrow but Jon was having problems. Several times she caught him as he slid. Eventually she sat him behind her, put her saddlebags onto his pony and led it.

At some point in the early morning, she slid from her horse and threw up on the side of the road. Jon perched uncomfortably and managed to hold on, no more. Gavin dismounted to hold her head, uttering soothing comments about shock. He got a tiny fire going to make a warm drink, saying they could all do with something. The sickness subsided and she was left feeling hollow again.

They rode for a couple of days. Mika threw up each morning, regular as clockwork, until she could no longer deny she was pregnant. Gavin said nothing, she was sure he'd realised her condition, he wasn't stupid. He simply kept her eating and drinking, offering sympathy when needed.

Mika spent the time riding deep in thought. Jace would come after her, he must have realised what he'd smelt wasn't Lissina. He'd tried to get her to react as a boy, she wouldn't be safe anywhere as a girl and Gavin wouldn't say where they were going.

Jace - that cat he held with him, there was something about it that troubled her. The cat had been rampaging the countryside she'd been told and yet Ackbarr didn't have any big cats, they were endemic to Cassai. Belindros had thought she was her brother. Her thoughts spun round until she went cold and swore to herself for not seeing it before. If she could change into a cat, then why not her brother? Kaylan must have shamed her parents by not being able to control himself and turning into a cat. She wondered what they would think of her and shook her head, not wanting to think about it.

Belindros had said Jace could control others. Was he keeping Kaylan in that shape, forcing him to do his bidding? Her resolve hardened, she had to go back and get him free of Jace. Maybe she could help him regain control himself. She remembered seeing the other cats in the cage, pacing and staring. She shivered and noticing Gavin's eyes on her, tried to keep her face neutral.

Mika offered to take the last watch that evening, using the excuse that she woke early to throw up anyway. She slept dreamlessly in her blankets until Gavin shook her with a big hand, then sat, wrapped up next to the remains of the fire. The night was sparkling cold as she watched the moons over the hills. The breathing of the other two became regular.

She rose and spoke quietly to her horse. Gavin's black gelding pushed himself close, wanting attention too. He snorted as she shoved his nose away. After several days riding, he was still eager to go. She saddled her horse, wincing at every jingle and stamp of the horse's feet.

"What's up?"

"Nothing. Won't be long." She should have known Gavin would disturb at a sound.

Jon was curled in a ball leaning against Gavin, his breathing long and slow. Gavin couldn't move without waking Jon. He sighed and settled back down grunting,

"Be careful. If you're not back soon, then I'll come looking for you."

"Yes." She had no intention of coming back. She turned her horse towards Ackbarr and rode.

Mika came through the gates just before they closed. Her horse was tired and she slid off to lead it towards Ezra's place instead of home. He'd be worrying over her disappearance. She wondered if he'd gone to find Marta. She missed him with a sharp ache, needed the feel of his arms around her, to see the lazy look in his eyes and his fingers fiddling with the strings on his gitern.

She tied the horse up and climbed the stairs to his room. She waved away his neighbours asking if she'd seen him and unlocked the door. Everything was quiet inside, then an iron smell hit her nostrils and she cried out. Brown stains ran down the walls, the same nightmare she remembered from Fenin. There was blood everywhere. She staggered back against the door frame, only the cold weather had stopped it smelling further and alerting someone. A voice called from the stairs having heard her cry.

There were people talking, a friend of Ezra's pushing past her to get into the room and they took her downstairs. Further shouting and questions as more people found out, Ezra had been popular. A cup of something strong was pushed into her hand and she drank without thinking.

Mika watched the hustle around her with a growing anger, a coldness that made the hurt dim, locking it inside her. Only one person could have done this. He'd seen her dressed as a boy with Ezra in the park, clowning around and pretending to be mates. He was targeting the people around her that he could hurt. Belindros and his household were safe. The other Medici apprentices and the nobles were safe too. He'd isolated Lissina, how long before he found Jon?

She stood, ignoring the people pulling at her and left. Mika walked her horse home and tied it up in a silent dream. Images floated through her mind, nothing had been left in Ezra's room in one piece. Blood everywhere. His gitern smashed, clothes shredded. He'd put up a fight despite being a musician and not a swordsman. Mika hoped he'd hurt Jace somehow. Part of her brain was screaming that Jace meant her to confront him.

Mika slid into the house. It was quiet. Belindros was normally out at this point in the day and Marta in her rooms. A few servants looked her way curiously and she waved at them, hoping that they wouldn't know why she'd left or ask why she was back.

She looked in the dispensary. The list for Jace's drugs was there, she mixed them carefully and placed them in the boxes used. It was nearly the right time to deliver them, she could say Jace needed another supply, she was known well enough at the palace now for the excuse to be accepted. She watched herself adding a fatal ingredient to the mix, not caring about the consequences of her actions. Ezra was dead. Nothing else mattered.

There was a guard on Jace's rooms. After a brief hesitation she walked up and announced she had something for Jace. The guard looked at the box, recognised Belindros' seal and waved her into the antechamber to Jace's rooms without a comment. Jace opened the door to her knock. He was unshaven, bags under his eyes as though he'd not slept. His hand trembled on the door frame.

The guard blanched at the sight of him, "You are to remain in your rooms." He flushed as his voice cracked. She felt sorry for the guard, he wasn't much older than her.

Jace's mouth opened, she saw the sharp inhalation and his gaze swung to fix on her. He knew what she was. As if with a great effort, he pulled back the door and inclined his head to invite her in. The courtly gesture contrasted with his rumpled appearance.

In a dream she stepped through. The rooms inside were dark and musty, it wasn't fit to be an animal lair, no sane animal would live in a pit like this. He slammed the door shut behind them and leant against the wall, his arms folded.

"I've brought your drugs." He ignored her. She held the box towards him and he slapped it out of her hand.

He was staring at her intently, lips drawn back slightly, drawing her scent into him. "You aren't a boy." It was the first time he'd addressed her, his accent was Cassai, taking her back to her homeland. Jace shifted to one side and she moved away, realising too late that he'd blocked the door. He smirked, seeing her dismay.

"Where's the cat?"

He gestured. The cat was sprawled by the side of the room. Her brother - she reached out mentally to him and flinched as something brushed against her mind. The cat looked up, sniffing the air, mimicking Jace's movements. Something jagged slashed across her brain and she cried out.

"You're mine." She steadied herself to watch Jace, he was stalking her. Mika drew her sword and another pain slammed through her head, sickening this time. "I smelt you, not that foolish girl. I realised when I met her alone. You've been laughing at me, all this time."

"Why did you rape her then?" She could barely get the words out.

"Why not? An appetiser before the real pleasure of having you." He must be mad, Lissina's father was a well-regarded noble, raping his daughter for fun was suicidal. The twitch of his muscles warned her before he moved. He grabbed his own sword from a table and flicked the end her way. His eyes widened as she blocked him. The weight behind his sword drove her back.

Jace was frighteningly fast, his face set as he concentrated on breaking her defence. Mika shifted constantly to avoid his sword, sweat trickling down her back. She used every trick she could think of to keep him away. She had to keep watching him, needed to know what his next move would be and yet their eye contact made a connection between them. It was one he exploited to the full, staring her down, flicking his rapier while he mentally assaulted her. The sexual twisting inside her and against all reason, she could feel her body wanting to obey him.

Mika tried to remember Lissina, bruised and bloody, thought of the damage he'd done to her. Belindros explaining, "A cat's penis has barbs on it you know..."

He was male and without realising, her lips drew back and she breathed in his scent, strong in the stuffy room. There was something else too, another male. Her eyes were dragged away to look at the cat by the wall. It sat upright, staring at her in the same way as Jace.

A sharp pain and her hand involuntarily opened, dropping her sword. Gavin would have been disgusted with her. Jace had taken advantage and attacked, she fumbled to grab the hilt and missed. He held his sword at her throat as she backed away.

Jace bared his teeth, enjoying her discomfort and increased his psychic battering. She swayed and he reached out to smack her casually around the side of her head, fingers outstretched. She felt a slicing and realised with horror that his hand had claws on the end. Blood dribbled down the side of her face and a low growl came from the wall.

"Kaylan."

A whisper and the cat attacked, ears back, face a mask of fury. Jace shifted away, twitching his sword to keep Kaylan at a distance. His mental buffeting lashed out at her brother instead, giving her vital time to recover. She could feel how difficult it was for her brother to disobey. His movements were awkward, stilted. Jace's in comparison were languid, smooth, male… She shook her head, mustn't think that way. She staggered away from them, tripping over the clothes on the floor that tangled her feet.

Without thought she whimpered, a small hunted creature trying to hide from the predator playing with it. Too fast, Jace slammed her brother to the ground in mid spring. He whirled and smacked her hard as she stumbled from the backlash of emotions, knocking her against the wall and her knees buckled.

Confident Mika would stay where she'd fallen, Jace strode over to her brother, intent on finishing him off. Kaylan crouched, unable to resist. She fumbled for her knife and launched herself at him with the last of her strength. Caught by surprise, Jace was knocked off balance and dropped his sword. Blood bloomed against his clothing from the slash she'd made in his back and she had a brief glimpse of Kaylan lying on the floor with a huge wound in his side. She'd failed, Mika sagged in defeat. She scented the iron tang of blood, another distraction she could do without.

A hand grabbed her and she was swung around as Jace used her to pull himself upright. He leaned against her, staring down into her eyes, twisting the knife out of her hand. His eyes were huge in the dim room, drawing her in. The pupils weren't entirely round, they widened and slitted.

Mika had no space left for anything, not her brother, not herself. She fell into his eyes, trapped by the nearness of his body. Of their own volition her hands clenched, kneading the warm hard muscle under her hands. What was left of Mika's mind screamed at the betrayal of her own body wanting him. His scent all around, inches away and his hands shifted to around her throat. He battered at her mentally, forcing her to become aware of him and his wants.

Mika couldn't breathe, he was strangling her, using her lack of air to break her will. Blackness in the edges of her vision, her sense of self crumbled and she started to stretch and yawn into the change. A wild exhilaration to the emotions whirling around them, her skin trembling.

His eyes widened further, a gasp choked out and the mental assault stopped dead. She inhaled sharply as cold reality drenched her and his hands left her throat. He was staggering back, fighting something. Kaylan had hold of him, pulling him to the floor. The cat was shaking the tall man, gripping him by the nape of his neck. Jace was unable to do more than utter a thin keen, scraping impotently at the cat on his back. Blood was flowing from Jace, flowing from the cat, swirling together in streaks on the floor.

Mika fumbled, scrabbling for Jace's rapier, wobbled as she tried to aim and missed. Jace jerked again, face twisted in pain, bloody rents opening up under her brother's claws. This time she got it right, a last convulsion and he was still. Kaylan continued to worry at him as Mika slumped to the floor.

She stared as her brother slowly lost interest in Jace, panting as he licked the large wound in his side. Blood dripped steadily.

"Kaylan."

He growled as she tried to move closer. She stopped, noticing his eyes, lambent in the dimness. He appeared exhausted, yet she was frightened to go near him. Male. She shook her head, unsure what she felt. A pressure coming from him. With horror she recognised the same compulsion she'd had from Jace.

They stared at each other. Nothing moved in the stuffy room, only the trickle of blood staining his skin darker. Every trick she'd learnt in controlling herself in the last few months she used, desperately trying to stay conscious as Mika. She panted in exhaustion and fought the sensation to change, battening down the crawling of her skin. Kaylan weakened and the impulse faded as he forced out a moaning chirrup.

She could feel how exhausted he was, how the wound pained him and yet every time she shifted, he would growl, determined to keep her in place. Eventually he slid to one side, sprawling onto the floor, his eyes closing. He nuzzled at his wound. She knew from her studies it would be fatal if not treated, but she couldn't get close to him. His head flopped and he rallied himself to warn her to stay still again.

The door banged, Kaylan pulled himself upright with a huge effort and collapsed into a heap. Gavin ran in, sword in hand, followed by Belindros and Jon.

Belindros looked at Gavin and indicated Jace, "Deal with him." He walked around Kaylan and blocked her view of both her brother and Jace.

"It's Kaylan. He's the cat, Jace had him all this time. He won't let me help." Her voice dried up. Belindros nodded, his hands gentle as they began to check her over. Mika relaxed into his ministrations and closed her eyes.

A trail, spreading like a stain in water, tickled the edges of her mind. She watched it, passively waiting, too tired to fight anymore. It demanded something of her and she moaned deep in her throat, skin trembling. Belindros raised her eyelid, checking something. Jon hovered watching them anxiously.

"Gavin?" His voice calm, Belindros turned slightly, pointing to her brother. Relaxed, Mika lay still, re-closing her eyes, Gavin would help Kaylan. Mika closed her eyes and felt the presence grow stronger, warmer. Her brother felt close by and she welcomed him without thinking. She drunkenly stretched as the insidious tendrils coaxed her to change.

A tearing wrench in her mind drenched her into sobriety. She almost threw up into Belindros' lap and clawed her way upright. Jace lay by the bed, looking curiously small, until she realised he was missing his head. Her gaze swung to the naked figure of a young man lying on the floor close by. His features were stamped with her likeness, his hands curled into claws.

Kaylan and blood was pouring from his throat. Gavin crouched over him, knife in hand.

Mika's head began to whirl, not Gavin, not this. Kaylan... She grabbed hold of Belindros, pulling at him, began to rock, her mouth open. Caught off balance, Belindros nearly fell into her.

He looked sharply at Gavin, "Get her out of here." Gavin opened his mouth to question and he snapped, "I can deal with this now. Anyone else risks the King's disfavour."

Mika was dragged by Gavin, protesting and crying, desperately trying to see her brother. Outside in the antechamber, Gavin shook her, making her teeth chatter. "You need to walk out of here normally, for everyone's sake. Lin will deal with things, you have to trust him."

"You killed him." It came out as a shrill whisper, the pressure in her head was intense. She shook again, a deep noise coming out of her throat.

Gavin set the point of his knife against her neck. His face was calm. "You change and I will kill you." She shuddered, her skin beginning to crawl. Her lips peeled back, the knife pressed harder.

"Mika, please, I don't want to do this, but I will." He shoved her back against the wall, "Mika." His voice came from a distance, the call of the forest louder.

A bang and a scuffle at the edge of her conscious vision, "Mika!" It was Jon, his shrill voice pierced the forest glade she walked through. He grabbed her, ignoring Gavin's blade and wrapped himself around her, "Please, do as he says. I need you." She gazed down, the call fading, deeper breaths gasping through her lips as she dragged herself back from the edge. He took her hand, "We need to walk out of here."

She nodded drunkenly, content to do as he asked. Gavin took the knife away, though he remained wary. They walked out of the palace, she staggered and nearly fell as the fresh air hit her. Gavin kept her upright and marched her back to the house.

Chapter 21

They followed the edge of the mountains. Coming off the main road, they passed through the foothills in the wild country east of Ackbarr. Gavin hunted to supplement their supplies. Mika tried not to see the dead animals he caught and forced herself to eat the meat. Jon's riding improved until he could ride his pony without Mika worrying about him falling off. Gavin kept the pace slow after the first day, pandering to her mood and Jon's inexperience.

Mika felt exhausted, bone weary. She refused to speak to Gavin, accepting his help because she had to, no more. Tight with anger at the betrayal of Belindros, grieving for her brother and Ezra and her worry over Lissina. All that kept her going was her baby, her last connection with Ezra. It forced her to stay with Gavin. She had nowhere else to go, no way of surviving on her own.

She threw up every morning. Gavin hauled her back onto her horse each time and fed her tiny amounts of food to keep her going. Jon got little more from her, she was aware of his worried face appearing at the side of her vision and the way he leaned against her at nights to keep her warm. She was unable to respond to his concern, deep in her own misery.

A series of buildings appeared on the horizon after ten days of travel. Larger than the usual village or hamlet and with an order about them unusual to a place of that size. The scenery had opened up, there was a salty smell in the air and the clouds brought a steady drizzle that soaked and chilled. As they rode through the shallow valley towards the settlement, she noticed it didn't have the feel of a town or village. There were very few fields, although plenty of large barns for stock and storage. The population felt transitory, a multitude of tents surrounding the main buildings.

Gavin left to speak to someone. Mika sat, staring blankly, the horse restive under her. She let it crop the pale winter grass and Jon moved his pony close to hold her hand.

"It's up this road, not far now." Gavin had returned. She looked away, not wanting to acknowledge him.

On the cliff was an arching stone bridge soaring into the side of the mountain. Turrets pointed skywards, the huge building looked insubstantial and delicate, the only access up a steep path. Below, the sea roared, crashing against the bottom of the cliffs, the spray leaping high into the air. She'd never seen the sea before. It seemed restless to her, in constant motion, she couldn't take her eyes away.

"The Temple Library. It's one of the few places where men are only tolerated." Gavin smiled as they started to climb the steep incline to the bridge. "Even the King hesitates before upsetting the priestesses."

The word got through to her. "Priestesses?"

"That's the best way I can describe them, although it's not strictly accurate. The priestesses are tolerated in Ackbarr, similar in some ways to how Cassai is. They've always threatened to burn the great library rather than allow the knowledge to fall into anyone else's hands. A large majority of them are healers. In times of crisis they travel to help, otherwise they stay within a certain radius of the citadel."

Gavin was delighted to have her finally showing some interest. "They have so many books here Mika. A person could spend a lifetime learning in the library and never read everything. I've been here with Lin before. The Medici support them, sending any further knowledge to their library to be filed for safekeeping. The priestesses tolerate them inside the library, but not within the complex itself. Wait until you see it, you'll like it here."

Halfway up they dismounted to lead the horses up the switchback trail. A small opening at the end of the bridge, large enough for a horse, no bigger. Several guards stood waiting, she noticed there was something odd about them. When one spoke, she realised, they were women, nearly the same size as Gavin. Mika surprised herself as a pang of jealousy darted through her lethargy.

They stopped in the large courtyard, Mika could still smell the ocean, a clean ozone. It cleared her head as she waited, making her sit up and look around in a way she hadn't for days. Gavin jumped down, held Jon's pony and offered a hand to Mika. She ignored it and slid down to watch two women approaching them.

One took the horses and the other beckoned them to follow. Mika gazed around as they walked through the corridors. Most of the figures she saw were women, dressed in the same grey robes as their guide.

They were brought into a study, cosy with a small fire burning to keep the chill off. Their guide murmured their names and left them. They were met by a tall grey haired woman, lines deep in her face.

"I am Chiara, head of the Temple Library. I am told Belindros sent you to me?"

Gavin inclined his head, "Madam, I have brought Mika to you. She is Belindros' apprentice. Belindros wishes you to look after her for a while. I have a letter explaining."

He passed it over and there was a long silence while she read. Jon fidgeted while Mika stared at the books on the shelves and wondered if she'd get a chance to read any.

Eventually Chiara looked up at Mika, "You will be as one of us. Dress in our clothes, do the same work."

"I'm pregnant."

She inclined her head, "You wish to keep the baby?"

Mika's mouth dropped. The thought hadn't crossed her mind. It was the only part of Ezra she had left, how could she not want it? She fenced the grief back in where it belonged and whispered, "Yes."

"We will find duties for you that are not too onerous. You were Belindros' apprentice, you may continue your learning here. That is what he has suggested as a cover. Many come to study with us."

Mika gritted her teeth, she wasn't keen on this woman. She found her pompous, but she still wanted to learn. "May I leave if I wish?"

"If you wish. You are not a prisoner here. The child may stay with the younger children in the complex. You warrior, will need to stay in the dormitory next to the hospice in the valley if you wish to stay."

Gavin refused, "With respect Madam, I will only stay tonight. I have promised to return to Belindros."

They were waved out of the study with little ceremony. Gavin walked back to the courtyard and Jon dragged Mika with him, wanting to say goodbye. When they reached the courtyard, Jon clung to Gavin as he swept him into his big embrace.

"You will be safe here Mika." She felt Gavin's gaze on her. She couldn't react, torn between their previous friendship and her memories. Mika turned her head away, seeing images of her brother under his knife.

She watched as Gavin led his horse out of the gate and out of sight, Jon sniffing beside her. Another person appeared beside them to lead them to their new rooms. Jon was shown to his quarters close to the courtyard and Mika promised to come and see him as soon as she'd been shown hers.

Her room was smaller than her room in Ackbarr, more austere. A set of grey robes lay on the bed, she refused to wear them for the moment. The thought of conforming dragged her spirits down. She opened the shutters and looked out towards the sea. A spray of damp greeted her and the endlessly moving animal down below, a restless mass of grey. Little could be heard over the wind whistling and the roaring of the sea.

Her face healed, leaving four long scars down the side and a large nick close to her eye. She was lucky she was told by the healer, not to have lost it. Her stomach grew rounder, a little at a time. Her anxiety over losing her baby never quite left her, despite the constant attentions of those skilled in childbirth. The sickness in the morning stopped and she began to make friends with the younger priestesses. She let her hair grow, having to flick it out of her eyes and not worrying about bleaching it.

Concerns about the birth began to affect her, her dreams centred around finding a place to nest and hide, less of hunting. Despite Gavin's words, she never quite felt safe. She wanted to be at home and with a shock realised she thought of Ackbarr as being her home, not Cassai. She missed the bustle of the streets, the singing in the house and longed to go back, despite still being angry with Belindros.

Mika was fidgety, wanting to lash out for no reason. Worried about changing, she'd asked for a lock on her door and after sharp words with Chiara, she'd been allowed one. She endured interviews with scholars about her changing and insisted on seeing what was written down about her, correcting any speculations. They had little information on her kind, it appeared any information was jealously guarded by her people. She was unable to change when they asked, despite the irritation she felt something stopping her and wondered if it was to do with her pregnancy.

Her belly swelled, Jon commented with amusement on the number of times she went to the privy. She lectured him in return on the consequences of enjoying himself with girls, making him squirm in embarrassment.

Mika worked down in the hospice helping those who came. They'd bring food, money, whatever they could afford. If they could reach the hospice then they would be treated, no one was turned away. She took turns in weeding the gardens and cooking food. For the first time she enjoyed the company of women as a woman.

She watched the guards training and realised if she'd known of this place then she could have found sanctuary after Fenin. She wondered, if having had the choice between coming here or being in Ackbarr, what she would have chosen.

She sat in the library with Jon, helping with his studies or rather staring at the same book as him, until he jabbed her with a sharp elbow to remind her of the question he'd just asked.

"You're mooning again, it must be that baby."

Mika glared and he pulled a face to show how she'd looked two seconds ago. She laughed and stopped, a ghost from months ago stood in the doorway. Thinner than she had been, Lissina stood with one hand raised to her mouth in shock as she recognised them. Mika couldn't stop the guilt rising in her eyes and she started to stand, to say something, anything. Lissina turned and walked out of the room.

Jon looked confused, "Who was that?"

"Lissina"

He opened his mouth and shut it again as he realised. Relief that Lissina had recovered from her injuries filled Mika, followed by her own guilt. What was she doing here? How was she going to cope with Lissina being here? Her hands crept down to her stomach. She was pregnant, Lissina must have realised she was a girl. She sat slowly, feeling sick.

"What are you going to do?"

"I don't know."

At the main meal Mika saw Lissina again, despite Mika trying to stay behind the others. Lissina's eyes flicked to her and away constantly. She looked drawn, no longer the vivacious girl Mika remembered. Mika stood with the rest of the women at the table, hugely conscious of her stomach. She ate little and excused herself early. She stopped in the library to pick up a book she'd left earlier.

"Mikon." Mika turned, Lissina stood behind her in the doorway, her eyes accusing.

Mika took a deep breath, "It's Mika and I'm sorry."

"You lied to me."

"I didn't mean..."

"You lied to everyone, I'll tell them, tell all of them back in Ackbarr." There was a desperation in her words that Mika's heart bled to hear. Lissina's eyes widened as they dropped to her stomach. "You're having a baby."

"Yes."

"Is it...is it his?" She was trembling, fists clenched.

"No."

"How can you be pregnant then?"

How could she be pregnant? A number of cutting replies bubbled up and the only true one swamped them. "He killed Ezra."

"Ezra?"

"He was a musician." Mika's voice choked, "Jace killed him." Lissina flinched at the name. Mika longed to have some comfort, some feeling of sympathy between them. They'd been friends, they'd both lost something to Jace, surely they could...

Lissina's voice was cold, breaking through her thoughts, "I thought I loved you. You used me like everyone else."

"No."

They stood, looking at each other. Mika tried again, "Lissi, several years ago I was..."

"Shut up!" Lissina screamed. "Don't ever call me that again. Do you want to know what it was like? How he laughed when I begged him to stop..." Her words trailed off and her eyes glazed.

"He's dead." Mika's voice was small. "He won't hurt you again. I killed him."

Lissina's voice was flat as she replied, "He'll never be dead. Every time I close my eyes, I see him over me. Every night..." She paused, eyes squeezed tightly shut, fists clenched. Mika took a step towards her and she whirled out of the doorway, the sound of her steps unsteady through the long corridor.

The temple complex wasn't large. Mika kept seeing Lissina at a distance. Miserable, she tried to keep out of her way. Mika could see how unstable Lissina was, at some points she still didn't quite see her as a girl, despite her pregnancy. At others, Lissina accused her wildly of using her as cover. The look in Lissina's eyes if she caught sight of her in the dim corridors was horrendous, Mika wasn't sure at times if she was mistaking her for Jace. She attempted to speak to one of the priestesses and all she could counsel was patience.

Mika stomach had grown hugely in the meantime. Jon became solicitous beyond his years, running to get things for her, despite her protests that she wasn't an invalid. She longed to be slim and quick again, to move without thought. The healer watched her constantly, eyes narrow, making Mika more nervous every time she saw her. Avoiding Lissina one lunchtime, Mika walked through the courtyard seeing a swirl of horses, yet more visitors. She watched with interest, people came and left every day.

Then she caught the sight of a familiar silhouette - it was Gavin. He was helping someone down from a horse and her heart thumped as she recognised

216

Belindros. He was scanning the courtyard, looking. When he saw her, he raised a hand in greeting. Without thinking, Mika cupped her hands around her stomach and kept her distance while they collected themselves and walked away to greet Chiara.

Chapter 22

Belindros had been given rooms in the main part of the complex, for some reason they seemed to think that his age made him trustworthy around women. Mika snorted, she could imagine his comments about the plainer of the women here.

She knocked on Belindros' door, she'd come to see him reluctantly when he'd sent a message. She couldn't ignore him after all he had done for her, but she couldn't forgive his treatment of her brother. He opened the door and his eyes widened at the size of her stomach. A twist went through her. He must have known of her pregnancy, Gavin would have told him.

"Mika." He nodded her to a chair opposite him.

She remained standing, despite her aching back, "You wanted to see me Medici?"

His eyes glinted with anger, "You think I don't care? Try this one, you loved your brother, didn't you?" She nodded stiffly. "Could you have denied him the way you did Jace?" Mika looked startled. Denied him? "He'd been in that body too long Mika. Neither of us knew what state his mind was in. Could you have taken the chance that he wouldn't have taken advantage of you? The same way Jace wanted to?"

"He was my brother." She whispered it, not wanting to remember the tickling of a mind across hers, the warmth seducing her.

"Jace was your father." She shook her head as he continued, "Yes he was, he raped your mother and narrowly escaped being gelded for it. The man who brought you up wasn't your father. Why do you think

218

your mother never left the compound, except to see the few family members who would still talk to her? She couldn't risk Jace getting his hands on her again. Jace and your mother had the same grandfather. Complete bastard by all accounts."

"She told me..." She stopped, her mother had told her that she and her father were too closely related, that was all. Mika remembered her father's face while she'd spoken, blank and tight. Something clicked in her memory, all those months ago, the conversation between her parents she'd overheard. Her mother's stance in the moonlight.

"I don't know what she told you. All I know is that Koren did some fast talking to marry your mother so quickly. He was skilled in that even as a youngster." Changing the subject, he reached back to the table. "I brought these for you, I thought they might help."

She took the packet he held out, a familiar smell wafted up. "Dried vineflowers."

"Corettle is the proper name for it, vineflower is the native term. The Cassai use them to prevent the change happening."

She remembered the vineflowers twining around their house and garden. "Mother used them to keep us safe."

"Yes, I realise now. I know she used them."

Her feet hurt and she sank into the previously scorned chair. "What do you mean?"

"Your mother could change. Do you remember me telling you there was one woman alive who was capable of breeding true changers?" She nodded.

"That was your mother. Somehow Koren managed to fool the elders into believing you and Kaylan were his. He told me this when we met while he was looking for your brother. They'd thought you were both too old for a first changing. Thought you were safe."

Tears began to roll, "Why did they marry me off then? If they knew Kaylan had changed, didn't they think?"

He shrugged, "I don't know, things were happening too fast. Maybe they couldn't stop the marriage, it had been arranged previous to Kaylan's changing. Maybe they thought you'd be safer in Fenin." Her back ached and she shifted to relieve it. They sat in silence, not quite companionable. Mika was still wary, not entirely ready to forgive.

Belindros' voice was soft. "Mika, your brother was beginning to heal already. You seemed to be responding to something, your eyes were changing. Can you blame me for not wanting to take the chance? I knew you couldn't have denied him. You couldn't even stop that little twerp Orai from misbehaving." His whole body had slumped, "If he'd dominated you, then we'd have had two cats in the room, uncontrollable. Gavin couldn't have kept us safe. Jace's body was also attempting to heal."

"That's why you cut his head off?"

"Yes. I'm sorry you had to see that."

"He was my brother..." Her face was in her hands now, the tears streaming. Belindros pulled a stool close to her, carefully lowering himself onto it and held his arms out. Unable to deny herself the comfort, she fell into them and let him hold her while she sobbed. Gradually she became aware that her whole body was taut and uncomfortable, the baby inside her kicking out in protest. She rubbed her stomach.

"Forgive me?" The lines in his face were deep as he peered up at her.

Mika nodded, "How did you explain it all? The King couldn't have been happy."

"I did some very fast talking and thankfully the King acknowledged Jace was getting out of control. I don't think he was even taking the drugs I gave him properly anymore. Lissina was the last straw. The others had been serving girls, beneath the King's notice. Lord Dellon, Lissina's father, was applying pressure to get rid of him, plus the others of the court who weren't happy."

"And Ezra?" Her voice nearly crumbled again.

"Ezra is being missed by everyone who knew him well."

She bowed her head. Belindros waited until she asked, "What excuses did you make?"

"Something along the lines that you'd brought his drugs instead of me and he'd lost control of his cat. It helped that the guard had seen you come out with claw marks down your face."

"Why didn't he come and help? He must have heard all the noise."

Belindros snorted, "Don't blame him, he was only a young lad. Jace terrified him, you'd seen him fighting. That guard was more of a sop to the nobles demands. If Jace had wanted to get out then he would have. Gavin shoved his way past that lad with barely a protest, he was only too pleased to have someone else take control."

"Lissina is here."

He nodded, "I'd have warned you if I'd known. Her father told me before I left. It must have been a shock, for both of you. How is she?"

"I don't know. Her body seems to have healed but not her mind. She's accusing me of everything."

The lines in his face settled deeper and he said quietly, "I wonder sometimes if surviving is a good thing. I'll speak to her and see what I can do."

There was a long silence between them, the fire crackled and hissed from the salt in the wood. Far outside, the sea could be heard, crashing against the cliffs below.

Belindros stretched and moved back to his chair. "Your father – Koren, took both of them back to Cassai. They've held the funeral."

"Including Jace?"

"He was royal. In some ways, by being able to change, more than most."

"Why didn't you tell my father I was with you?" She still thought of her father as the man who'd raised her. She shied away from thinking of Jace as her father.

"Politics." Belindros' voice was disgusted. "I couldn't be seen talking or sending messages to him. The King wanted Cassai isolated, to help him persuade his nobles that they could invade. They knew I'd been there on many occasions and I had you as an apprentice. All I could do was allow Koren to see you. I thought it would help. I didn't know you weren't Kaylan."

"Why have you come here?" Her hands cradled her stomach, the last worry left.

He nodded at her hands, "To help you. I thought it might help if you had someone around during labour that you knew..." Uncharacteristically he trailed off.

She let him simmer, then said simply, "I'd like that."

He beamed and Mika realised how worried he'd been, how unsure of her reactions.

With Belindros around, the days settled into a rhythm, it was back to learning again and with a contentment that hadn't been there before. Belindros regained his acerbic wit, whilst looking out for signs of tiredness from her and Jon was whipped into shape. Mika would sit back at times and watch them bickering happily. The summer turned into autumn, the sea changing from deep blue in the sunshine to a sullen pewter grey. Mika's stomach grew more enormous and Gavin teased her about stealing his food. Lissina appeared to respond to Belindros' help. He said she'd been found duties helping others down at the hospice.

The few times Mika saw Lissina were still too many, both of them coming to a halt in the corridor if they saw each other. Mika deliberately kept her eyes down at mealtimes in case she caught Lissina's gaze. The last month of pregnancy was especially bad. Feeling heavy and uncomfortable, Mika spent more time gazing out of the window in her room than walking.

Mika lay in bed, two small bundles next to her. Jon hovered, fascinated by the movement of the sleeping babies. The birth had been long and frightening for both her and Belindros. He'd not allowed anyone else in the room during the labour and they were both exhausted by the end of it. Neither of them had known how she would react to the stress.

She lay in her bed for several days, moping about her room. Never having been good at boredom, she struggled to the library, sat and read in between feeding the babies. To her frustration, she discovered she couldn't go anywhere with them, the two together were too much and Jon had to help. With the frustration of her tired body, her mind kept driving her on, unable to stop herself. Exhaustion beckoned as she found herself staring at the same page, not having read any of it.

The care of her babies was an endless cycle of feeding, changing and washing. Mika having expected to turn back into her old self immediately after the birth, was thwarted by them waking during the night and her own body refusing to do as she wished. She was offered assistance and she refused, believing she had to do everything for them herself. She imagined Ezra's reactions, half asleep at night while feeding them, not realising he would have laughed and told her to accept the help.

Depression grew and her other side began to wake. The dreams began again, frightening her with their intensity. She felt torn between the love she had of her independence and learning, and the fierce love she had for her babies. They were stocky limbed and dark haired, neither appeared to take after her for the moment. Even Belindros had shrugged at her questions. She would have to wait until they'd grown to see if they'd inherited her curse or his gift of music. Her thoughts ranged further ahead - ten or fifteen years of waiting, she'd nearly be in her thirties and her thoughts plummeted further as she saw her life narrowing in front of her.

"I'm worried I'll hurt them." The confession came out several weeks after the birth as Belindros sat in her room one evening, the babies in their basket. "I've been having those dreams again, I don't seem to be able to control when they happen."

He looked thoughtful, "I don't think you'd hurt them, part of you would recognise them as yours, surely?"

"What if I don't?"

"Then put them in another room, we can get someone else to sleep with them."

His sensible answer infuriated her. "No!"

"You're looking tired, a good night's sleep..."

Mika ignored him, standing as one of the babies shifted, anticipating them wanting to feed again. Both healthy boys, they had an appetite their father would have been proud of. She was losing weight rapidly, dark circles under her eyes. She turned away sharply, Belindros watching with sympathetic eyes.

"Do you want to look after them?"

He'd put his finger on the one sore point she didn't want to think about. She put her head in her hands, "I love them, I just can't do anything, can't go anywhere. I can't even read, they feed constantly, wake in the night. I can't concentrate."

"It will change, they don't stay this small forever."

A whisper, "It'll be years."

"You could continue your studies at home, in Cassai. Your parents would love to have you back. There are plenty of healers who are women there. They would also be happy to have you here at the temple. I have heard nothing but praise from Chiara and the hospice. They'd find you a wet nurse and you could study further."

"Not to become Medici." There was a long silence. She'd finally said it.

"Is that what you want?"

She raised her head to look at him, "Yes." Mika felt a relief burst as she finally gave herself permission to voice her feelings. "Ackbarr is my home. I want to study with you."

Belindros' voice was quiet, "You know I would be delighted to have you back as Mikon. I wish you could be Mika there, but you know that is impossible. This has to be your choice. If it helps, I met your father when he came to collect the bodies and I told him of Gavin's suspicions. He came back with this." Belindros handed her a letter and left her to read it.

She read it and wept. A choice had to be made. To look after her babies or to go back into the world as a boy. The offer she'd been made meant they would never know her as their mother. She stared at them through the night, watching the movements they made, cuddling and feeding them.

Belindros left a week later having made the arrangements. Mika watched from the turret overlooking the cliff until he, Gavin and their entourage disappeared from sight. She worked that evening in a fog until she was ordered to bed. She lay alone, sniffing the vineflower sachet her mother had given her and longed for oblivion.

The next day Mika began training with a purpose, she threw herself into it, exhausting herself with every opportunity. She re-trained her muscles, tightening them from the slackness of pregnancy. The guards were only too pleased to have someone new to practise against, until they saw how she drove herself. She was advised to slow down and refused. She couldn't go back to Ackbarr like this, no one would believe she was a boy. Her milk dried up over a matter of weeks, she tied up her corsets and cut her hair. Mika met Lissina in the corridors, Lissina's eyes grew wide when she saw Mika and she flinched away. Mika strode on, steeling herself to ignore Lissina's face.

The dreams continued, she'd have to re-learn her control. She could only sleep with a vineflower sachet next to her. Several times she forgot and woke to find her room wrecked. They refused to let her out at night, so she walked down to the hospice with Jon in the morning and didn't walk back. That night she stalked through the woods hunting small creatures. The exhilaration made her wake crying and naked in the morning. She lay sniffing and shivering in the cold morning air.

She wasn't entirely sure where she was. A few landmarks made sense, she picked her way through the woods, heading for the sea and heard Jon shouting for her. He'd ridden down with spare clothes and looked embarrassed at her nakedness when he found her.

Chiara tried to keep her inside and eventually gave into Mika's demands, giving her the use of a locked courtyard to change in. Mika tested all the shutters, she didn't want herself to break out. She had spectators from amongst the scholars the first night, peering from a window high up. They didn't return for a second night and flinched when she passed them. The changing helped, the tension leaked away and she began to feel honed, a fighting machine, the confidence of a predator infusing her.

It was iron winter by the time Mika and Jon started back. Jon rode next to her, cheerfully singing out of tune, delighted to be out of the restrictive surroundings. They'd wanted her to stay at the temple, tried to find excuses, offered rewards. She'd refused them all. The long conversation she'd had with Chiara had been exhausting. She didn't want to think about her reasons for leaving or the consequences. She'd given up

227

her babies for the chance to become a Medici, nothing less was going to stop her.

Epilogue

Mika was working in the palace hospice when another apprentice came to fetch her. She walked to Abran's office and found Koren waiting. She stopped herself, not Koren. He was still her father and despite her new knowledge she refused to think of him as anything else. Mika stood and stared as Abran murmured a few pleasantries and left them. The door was open and her father left it open, a servant waited further down the corridor.

"I have come to tell you that your mother is pleased with you." His eyes were pleading under the calm tone and impassive face. "She is out of confinement and has had two baby boys delivered."

Her babies, her mother had them. They would be safe, she closed her eyes in relief. "Thank you for letting me know." The audience in the corridor made both of them formal, the stiffness belied the looks they gave each other. They couldn't even speak in their native language, so much was suspect.

"I have heard from Abran that you are doing well in your capacity as a healer. You do your family and country credit. Many who come under your hands will think twice about the rumours they have heard."

She longed to rush into his arms, wanting to reassure him that he was still her father and hating the lie they both had to live. Keeping her voice steady, she replied, "Thank you. Please let my mother know I wish her well."

Her father nodded and bowed, "I look forward to hearing of your progress." She watched as he walked away, part of her heart going with him.

Brooding in her room later on, her eye was caught by the piece of paper in a crack of the wall, close to the ceiling. She smiled at the memory. Jon had been complaining, not understanding why reading and writing were so important.

"All those books in Belindros' study. They have the knowledge of other Medici in them. You can find out by reading."

His face had screwed up, "Belindros says it's all crap."

She tried to explain, "It's like having a conversation with someone from a long time ago. Sometimes the information they give isn't quite right or things have changed, but it's useful anyway. Belindros keeps a journal of everything he's learned, one day that might be thought crap too." Jon's eyes grew wide at anyone thinking of Belindros like that. "He wants us to use our heads, not blindly follow, do you see?"

Seeing that he wasn't entirely convinced, she carried on, "Look, if I write your name on this piece of paper and put it up here, then one day someone will discover it, maybe after you've died. That's the power of writing. Maybe one day you'll write a book people will want to read." He fell over on her bed laughing, tickled by the thought of him writing a book, but over the next few days she'd caught him looking up at the crack with a thoughtful look on his face.

A bang brought her back to the present and Jon leaned around her door, "Found a new pie stall, fancy trying it out?" She grinned and shoved Jon out the way to race down the stairs with him following close behind.

*****

Thank you for reading!

More frog than princess, Erme Lander lives in Gloucestershire with her husband, two children and a mad cat.

For more books by Erme Lander, please go to -

www.ermelander.co.uk

www.ingramcontent.com/pod-product-compliance
Lightning Source LLC
Chambersburg PA
CBHW072232170626
46813CB00003B/1181